Along the Trail to
THUNDER HAWK

By

George Gilland (Brings Back Buffalo)

and

Sharon Daggett Rasmussen (White Dove)

ISBN: 1453666729
ISBN-13: 9781453666722

ČHÉTAN WAKÍNYAN

Ektá Ōhangleya Čhánku

e-CHA-h'dah
Tatanka Owichakuya kah
Wakinyela Ska

Foreword

All frontiers are places of transition where there are opportunities and losses. This is a story of opportunities and losses on the Dakota frontier in the early twentieth century as told to us by our fathers, grandfathers, mothers, and grandmothers. As the new century began, the Lakota Nation's mobile domination of the Great Plains had faded, the cattle barons' control of the open range had lessened, and the American republic was parceling out land in neat square packages. Immigrants straight from the Old World and by way of established eastern and southern states arrived at this internal North American frontier encouraged by the railroad company's effusive promotions. Emigrants from within were encouraged by the government agencies to settle on one piece of land and become farmers and ranchers. During this brief time when the energy of many cultures was melding to form one new and different America, a new and different kind of American who was both Lakota and *wasicun* (white) was formed.

We tell the stories of Robert Gilland (Red Eagle) and Brave Bear from the memories passed on to us from our families. Our generation is the last to be close enough to Red Eagle's times to be part of a pre-electronic oral storytelling tradition, and we have attempted to tell his story in his authentic voice. We are grateful that we listened to our fathers' stories over so many years. Although we tell this story as fiction so that we may try to capture our ancestors' voices, many of the facts, dates, events, and historical characters are supported by documents in the U.S. National Archives, the U.S. Supreme Court, and the *Aberdeen Daily News*.

We are the heirs of Red Eagle:
George Gilland (Tatanka Owichakuya), son of Robert Gilland
Sharon Daggett Rasmussen (Wakinyela Ska), granddaughter of Elizabeth Gilland Fero.
August 2010

Acknowledgments

We would like to thank the Standing Rock Sioux Joint Tribal Advisory Committee – especially JTAC Executive Director Luke Lopez – for generously supporting this work and enabling us to complete and publish this novel. We dedicate this work to all Standing Rock Lakota—our ancestors, our generation, and most especially our heirs.

We are deeply indebted to Karen Murley for her undaunted encouragement and for her designer's eye and hand in creating the cover and the maps. We would also like to thank the many friends and family members who read the early drafts of our work and responded with enthusiasm and encouragement, including Damen Gilland, Sherry Gilland, Mildred Daggett, Dennis Daggett, Amanda Dubin, JoAnn Wells, and Anne Wolmeldorf. We are also grateful for generous assistance from the staff of the National Archives. It is my hope that my daughter Kirsten and granddaughter Madison will share this novel with their grandchildren.

Sharon Daggett Rasmussen
August 2010

Acknowledgments

Lakota has several dialects, and I've tried to use the right dialect for the person speaking. Some Lakota words I remember from my father and some words I learned from others. My father, who spoke with the "L" dialect, told most of these stories to me when I was growing up, and I have tried to relate them as they were told, using his voice and sense of humor. Other family and friends (including Uncle Jim Gilland, Aunt Sadie Defender, Paul Red Fox, Mary Helen Archambault, Babe and Snooky Goodreau, and Mike Murphy) spoke different dialects, so some words used here may be given in the dialects they used. Uncle Jim learned "book" Lakota and Dad often laughed at the way he pronounced the words. Mike Murphy and I neighbored for more than twenty years and a better neighbor couldn't be found. Snooky Goodreau loved to play penny-ante poker and we played many a game. If the pot was short, Snooky always put a player in even if he hadn't anteed up. I deeply appreciate knowing all of these dear people and express my gratitude to them and their families for being part of my life.

There were many others on the white side of the fence who were and are still good friends; many have gone to greener pastures, but some of us are still making do with the pasture we are in. I especially want to thank Rose Tidball's family for her book, *Taming the Plains;* it was a good resource for backing up memory. I tried to stay on the track of truth, and I hope it didn't offend anyone. I like to think we called a spade a spade and not a shovel, but please, you be the judge!

George Gilland
August 2010

Table of Contents

Prologue

We all just stood there trying to figure out what had happened. Each one of us was still holding his gun and there was a lot a whiskey-clouded talk and pointing going on about which bullet went where.

"I heard a lot of shots go off," Karl Hourigan said, his voice no louder than a chirp.

"Tom was aiming right for Bob," Felix Fly stammered, trying to show us with his shaky hand. As usual, Arthur didn't say much, but one thing for sure—Tom was lying dead on the ground. I figured if it was my bullet, it was self-defense, but I'd better try to catch up with Charlie Gayton and tell him what had happened. Charlie had made it back to McIntosh before I caught up with him. When I told him what had happened, he put me in a cell and left.

When he came back he said, "Bad news for you, Bob. I'm going to have to hold you for murder." I thought turning myself in would show him that I had nothing to hide and the boys would tell the whole story. The boys had scattered and each one had seen—or not seen—something different.

Now I was beginning to understand why Brave Bear said never trust the law. I should have hit the trail for the Hole-in-the-Wall or someplace—anywhere would have been better than turning myself in.

CHAPTER 1

Blackfoot Creek Ranch

Mrs. Two Kettles thought that Dad was going to suffocate all of us the night I was born. Dad was so worried we were going to freeze to death when the thermometer hit twenty below that he kept building up and building up the fire. Mrs. Two Kettles had helped deliver dozens of babies on the reservation, but in her many years she could remember only a few winters that were so cold. The log house Dad built on Blackfoot Creek near Oak Creek just south of Fort Yates was pretty solid, but as the wind whistled around outside, the dipper froze hard in the water bucket. That night Dad named me Robert after his father, but Mother said I was to be called *Wanbli Luta* (Red Eagle), so right away I had two names for the two parts of me. On January 11, 1889, we were in Dakota Territory on Indian land. By the end of that year most of the of the Great Sioux Reservation's nine million acres would be part of the new states of North and South Dakota.

My dad, Ben Gilland, had been a sergeant in the US Army, Company D, Seventeenth Infantry, for six years. The day after he was discharged, April 15, 1881, he and my mother, Elizabeth Red Bird McEldery, got married. They met at one of the dances at Fort Yates where Dad sometimes played the fiddle. Although you could dance with an enemy of the United States, you couldn't marry one and still be a soldier, so Dad mustered out, married Mother, and took up ranching—he'd seen the opportunity to make a living raising livestock on the reservation. The family could run four hundred head of cattle or horses on the reservation rent free. Any over that number, they had to pay the same rate as the big cattle companies that had begun leasing up the whole reservation to run cattle on.

My folks raised cattle and horses from then on, and kids to help take care of them cows and horses. There were eight of us kids. Sadie was the oldest, then Annie, Ben, me, and then Edward. I couldn't say Edward when I was little and called him Ted or Teddy, so the rest of the family called him Ted too. Ted and I were really close and we were always doing things together, but he died when I was about fourteen. We were at the Indian boarding school over by Mandan when he died. He just, got sick one day and never got over it. Mother said he either had bad food or his appendix was broke. I thought maybe he ate too much soap at that Indian school. Then there was Abe, Bessie, and the youngest was Jim. Ben was my big brother and we did a lot of things together, but I sure missed Teddy.

Life was pretty easy. I played a lot with Ted and Annie. Ben was four years older than me and he seemed to always get to do the things I thought I wanted to do. But I soon learned that the things he was doing was more in the line of work and weren't all that much fun. We all got to go with Mother picking berries to make *wo'japi* (pudding) and help dig *TE-p'see-lah* (wild turnips) for stew. Mother dried these in the sun to last through the winter. Ted and I got to fetch buckets of water from the creek and pick up firewood from along the banks where the cottonwoods and oaks grew thick. In those days, before farmers and settlers started cutting the trees, wood was easy to find and there was lots of brush growing in the draws.

Lakota camp near Fort Yates about 1900.

It was a day's drive with a team and wagon to get supplies—about thirty miles one way either to Fort Yates or over to the town of Evarts from our place. It was a big event for us kids, because we all got to go along and we usually got to stay overnight with friends. It seemed like there were always some other kids to play with on our stays, and we most generally got hard candy and sometimes, even real fruit. But we never went for supplies but about three times a year.

We had some neighbors, and we did visit back and forth quite a bit. Our neighbors then were mostly Indians, but there was Mr. and Mrs. George Reed who had a log house not too far from us. They were missionaries from back east—Springfield, Massachusetts—and Mother got to be good friends with them. They soon moved over to Fort Yates and started a church, but they were back to our area frequently and Mother helped teach them how to say things in Indian. They converted her to the Christian religion, and our whole family were soon Christians. We were baptized into the Catholic Church, and that got us into the Catholic Indian School at Fort Pierre.

When it came time for me to go to school, Dad hitched up the team and drove us in the buggy over to the Fort Pierre Indian Boarding School. Sadie, Ben, and Annie had been there before, but it was my first time. Ted was too little to go and I sure missed him that first year away from home. We had to leave real early in the morning to get over to that school by evening. It must have been sixty miles away. I remember thinking we weren't ever going to get there, but we finally got there. It took a lot of adjusting to survive that place. No one could talk in Indian, not even my oldest sister, Sadie, and she was most nigh grown. And right away all the boys had to get haircuts, and we had to wear funny clothes. We stayed in a big building with a lot of beds at night and had to go to classrooms in the daytime, and there was a big kitchen and a room where we sat at long tables to eat. The school was an all-Indian school, but I remember thinking, we sure aren't learning anything Indian here.

Brave Bear was the first kid I met at that school. Dad had given me a sack of hard candy before he left, and I had taken a candy from my sack while I was waiting in line to get my hair cut. Brave Bear was standing behind me and had seen me take a candy, and said, "*Canhanp hanska etan maku wo* (give me some candy)."

"*Wanjie ecu wo* (take one)," I said. And he did, but one of those sister nuns heard us and right away grabbed each of us by the arm and took us outside to the pump and made us wash our mouths with soap and water. She told us we couldn't ever use those "savage" words ever again—we could only talk English at this Indian school.

Brave Bear and I were soon the best of friends—it made school a little easier having him there. That Sister Mary was always watching us, like a buzzard waiting for a sick animal to die. We called her the *Heca* (buzzard) when we seen her coming our way, but we made sure she was out of hearing range when we said it. Brave Bear lived with his mother—his dad had left one day and never came back. His dad was white too. His mother moved around a lot, living with different ones, and he didn't have much of a family life, so he went home with me several times. He even went with me to my mother's Aunt Wakinyela Ska*'s* (White Dove's), place over on the Rosebud Reservation.

Most of our neighbors were living in tepees when I was little, but over the years, Dad helped several of them build log houses. Dad was descended from Scotch pioneers who'd settled in Indiana, and his family there farmed and ran a blacksmith shop, so he knew some about both building and farming. He was so good at building things that some started calling him *Ben Tipi Wasté*, meaning "good house builder," and that name kinda stuck.

Dad had come to the Dakotas back in 1875 on the run. He had gotten into a fight out in Muncie, Indiana, and hit a prominent fellow of the community and that fellow was still out cold the next morning. Dad figured if that guy died, the people there would want to hang him. So he snuck out to the railroad tracks and jumped on a westbound train that ended up at Bismarck thinking that no one could find him there. He joined the army and was stationed at Fort Lincoln and later at Fort Yates. That fellow regained his senses right after Dad had left and was fine, so Dad wasn't wanted back in Indiana, but he didn't find out until about twelve years later. When he finally wrote his folks, he found out the guy he had hit had come to shortly after he had left and was OK. We did go back to Indiana for a few months when I was pretty young, and Dad even planted a lot of corn. I can still remember driving a team and walking behind a drag, dragging corn all day, but mother didn't like it out there so we came back to Dakota and home. I was glad to get out of Indiana too.

Besides ranching, Dad hunted game and sold it to the railroad crew that was putting in a new line west from Mobridge, so when I was home us boys got to go with him sometimes, and we always helped dress out his prey. Once he even shot a black bear. We were in the wagon and we could see something black under a thicket of plum trees. Dad had me hold the lines, and I got pretty scared; the team was pawing and prancy and wanted to run, and I thought they were going to run away, but I pulled back hard on them and they stayed put. Then Dad leaned on the back of the wagon and shot, and we had us a bear.

Mother had been born in the Oak Creek area in 1859. Her mother had married a white man, Samuel McEldery, when she was about four, so he was the only dad she could remember. Some say

Grandmother's first husband Bobtail Bull drowned in the Missouri River, but I heard others telling how he was shot by a gunman hunting Indians from a passing riverboat. Anyhow, she needed a husband and a father for her four little girls, and as one of the first fur traders on the Missouri, Sam was available. Another one said he traded some whiskey for a bale of hides and a pretty wife, but I doubt they were there at the time. Sam was another blue-eyed blond Scotchman from somewhere back east—I believe Mother said it was Johnstown, Pennsylvania. He had been a scout for the army, way back, and Mother had grown up around the Fort Yates area. All three of Mother's sisters—Annie, Fannie, and Mary—married men from the area and ranched on the reservation.

Mother could speak English but never did learn to read and write in English; she just never had an opportunity to go to school of any kind. I thought many times, why wasn't I so lucky? Schools had came to be when they put the Indians on reservations and us kids all had to go to what they called "Indian" schools. If we talked Indian at school, we got to wash our mouth with soap. We had to learn all the white ways and very little was taught about being Indian, and the stories that were written in books about Indians were completely different than the ones told by Mother and the relatives from her side of the family. Chief Gall, Chief Rain-in-the-Face, and Chief John Grass, were all her uncles, and my great uncles. Some of their stories were firsthand and I always felt they were a lot more likely to be the truth than what was written in books.

When I got out of school after my first year at Fort Pierre, Dad and the rest of the family had went to Wakinyela Ska's and built her a log house. Dad had gathered in a crew, and they built her a big log house along the White River a few miles from the Rosebud Agency. Mother's sisters and their families all came and we had quite a campout. My Aunt Annie had married John Powers, and their son Tom was about my age. Tom and I played together, but he wasn't the kind of friend Brave Bear was. He was always showing off and talking too much about himself. Aunt Annie and Uncle John's daughter May and my little sister Bessie were just babies then but they became the best of friends.

People said Aunt Mary was deaf and dumb, but I don't think so—she just didn't want to talk much. She married Joe Vermillion and they had two boys, Charlie and Arthur, about the same age as me and Ted. They didn't talk much either, and they kinda of stuck together rather than with the rest of us kids. Aunt Fannie married Frank Keefe and they had a son Frank Jr., but he was about as old as Sadie. Uncle John McEldery was there to help build Unci's house too; he was Grandfather Sam and Grandmother Elizabeth's only son. Uncle John moved around most of the time but he sometimes lived with Aunt Fannie and Uncle Frank. Even my other *Unci* (Grandmother) and *Tunkasila* (Grandfather) McEldery were there.

Dad made sure that log house was well built; it even had even an upstairs room where I got to sleep. The men cut and fitted the logs and filled in the cracks with heavy clay, then the womenfolk whitewashed the logs on the inside. When it was finished, everyone went home again, but I got left there the rest of the summer to help out.

I sure had some good times with Aunt Wakinyela Ska. She was my grandmother's sister from Mother's side of the family. Wakinyela Ska and Grandmother *Oblaya Kokeyahunla* (Prairie Chicken) were sisters and the daughters of an old chief called *Mahpiya Luta* (Red Cloud). Wakinyela Ska was living alone and was quite old, but she still carried herself well and I thought she must have been a very pretty princess in her day. Her family had mostly been killed in a massacre over at a place called Wounded Knee, and she needed help with getting food gathered up and wood piled up near her tepee for the coming winter, so Mother had sent me to help out. The best part of being with her was that we had to talk Indian because she couldn't talk a word in English.

It was real dry that summer so when Dad got back home, he moved the cattle and our home up north to a place on the Cannon Ball River, about thirty miles west of Fort Yates. There was already a house and corrals and some sheds there—it had been the old Patterson Cattle Company's camp, but they had quit the cattle business and just left, so it was vacant and Dad was the first to make it occupied again. It was a good layout for wintering cattle, but it sure was a lot farther from school.

During the winter, when a lot of the family was at my folks' for Christmas, they had made plans to take all of us boys to Wakinyela Ska's. She didn't want us to call her Wakinyela Ska; she was Unci to us, and even Brave Bear called her Unci. She was the nicest grandmother, always smiling and pleasant, and she always had only good things to say about anyone. And she was very clever at finding something to surprise us boys with. Brave Bear and I traveled to Unci's with Aunt Annie and Uncle John and our cousins. The Powers family lived over by the Cheyenne River Agency then so they picked us up at school on their way to Unci's. It was just Brave Bear and me that got to stay for the summer, though. No one thought Tom would be much help—even then he spent more time thinking of ways to get out of chores than doing them—and Brave Bear had nowhere else to go.

Unci was really happy to see us—her face lit up and her eyes just sparkled. She came right to me and gave me a big hug and a kiss on the forehead. I wasn't very keen about girls kissing me, but Unci was OK (she was my grandmother). She hugged Aunt Annie and the Powers kids and then stepped in front of Brave Bear, and said, "My, what a handsome young man! Wanbli Luta, *takeciyapi hwo* (what's his name)?"

"*Lel Mato Ohitika* (This is Brave Bear). He came to help me help you this summer," I said. Brave Bear got a hug too. He looked so surprised, like he'd never been hugged before. He gave Unci a big hug back and had a big smile on his face. I was soon showing Brave Bear all around and before I knew it, Unci said, "Boys! It is getting late, *oyunke iyehantu* (it is bedtime)." There were two boys upstairs and in bed, faster than two squirrels could climb a tree.

The summer was going fast—we had stacked a huge pile of wood by Unci's kitchen door and we had helped her pick baskets full of buffalo berries, wild plums, and chokecherries. Then one day Unci said that it would sure be nice to have some meat to dry so she could make pemmican. To make pemmican, dried meat was pounded with dried berries 'til it was a mixed pulp, then melted tallow was poured over it. It kept a long time and could be carried along on trips or added to a stew. It had a flavor all its own, rather good too!

"Do you think you boys could take my *winuhcala itazipa* (old woman bow) and shoot me a deer or an elk?" She handed me her bow and some arrows, then she brought out another one and handed it to Brave Bear, and said, "If Wanbli Luta misses, you might have to shoot the meat for Unci!"

She had shown me how to use her old woman bow last year, and I had gotten a big deer with it. To use an old woman bow, you had to sit down on the ground and place your feet against the big bow and pull the arrow back with both hands. Unci told of many times in her younger years of sitting below a buffalo jump and shooting wounded buffalo with her bow. The young men would stampede a herd of buffalo over a cliff, and the women and bigger boys would shoot the ones that didn't get killed in their fall off the cliff. She said that was back when the Buffalo Nation was about three million strong, before the white man came with their European diseases—chicken pox, smallpox, and measles—and their war on the Indians.

"We called ourselves People of the Buffalo Nation, but white men came along and started calling us Indians. We thought it funny at first—we knew we didn't come from India wherever that was. We had been natives of this place forever or as far back as any of the elders could ever recall. Now, many of the Buffalo Nation's people are gone and they are fast being replaced with white people," Unci told us.

I thought then where does that leave us? Maybe we are a new kind of people. People like Brave Bear and me—we are Buffalo Nation but we are white too. We know who we are but it sometimes confuses others, especially white people. In Indian school, we learned that it was good to be white, but from Unci we learned that it was good to be Indian. Unci said, "If you live like whites in the Buffalo Nation, then your heart is white, so the people of the Buffalo Nation will treat you as a white, and if you live the ways of the Buffalo Nation then you will be looked on as a native. That is the way of our people."

Unci told us how the Buffalo Nation had stretched from the Pipestone River in Minnesota to the eastern slopes of the Rocky Mountains, and from the Platte River in Nebraska to the Churchill

River in Canada. Seen through my boy-sized eyes, it seemed like we still had a lot of land. The two reservations together—Standing Rock and Cheyenne River—reached all the way from the Missouri River on the east, to the Cannon Ball River on the north, to the Cheyenne River on the south, and then it just stopped abruptly at a straight line to the west where some white man drew a line on a map just the other side of Black Horse Butte. Altogether, there was still about five million acres.

The thought of hunting put a big grin on Brave Bear's face, "Let's go get us a big elk!" We had seen deer and elk along the river, when we had hunted rabbits with our slingshots. The slingshots were a piece of round leather, about three inches across, with a leather string about a foot and a half long tied on each side. You put a rock in the pouch and held both strings and swung the pouch around, aimed at what you wanted to hit, and then let go of one of the strings. We didn't try hitting deer with our slingshots, but now we were equipped to hunt big game!

We decided to try our luck a mile or so down river from Unci's. We were coming upon a big grove of trees and we had seen fresh tracks not far away, so when we got to the trees, Brave Bear said that he would go around and come back through the other side of the trees and I could wait a little, then just walk straight in. So I waited about long enough to let him get around to the other side, then I started to ease into the thicket. It was tough going with a lot of willows and underbrush, but I was slowly making my way when I heard something coming. I thought, if that is Brave Bear, he must have ran all the way, but I sat down and put an arrow in the bow string, just in case it wasn't Brave Bear.

Coming at me not fifty feet away was a bull elk. I'd seen bigger, but he sure looked like he would do the trick, so I pulled the bow string back with both hands and aimed at his chest and let go. The elk was looking back when I shot and then he lunged forward and right at me. I thought I must have missed and I got scared in a hurry. He was about to run right into me, so I jumped up a little fast and dived behind a tree, and I didn't even take the bow with me. Lucky for me, I didn't need the bow—that elk just dropped to his knees and came down right where I had been sitting, and he died there. My arrow had went right through his heart. I got out my knife and cut its throat and had it gutted out in a while. It took me a lot longer than when I had hunted with my dad.

But no Brave Bear in sight. What is taking him so long to get through those trees? I decided I'd better go find him. I was about halfway through the trees when, there he was dressing an elk bigger than the one I had just killed. He was grinning all over and handed me a chunk of liver. I took a few bites, and then I asked about how he had gotten his elk. Talking fast, he told me that he had been chasing it through the trees, then suddenly it just turned around and headed right for him, so he had to just sit down and shoot it.

There was a couple of very excited boys running back to tell Unci. We told her all the details and she was just about as excited as we were. She said, "*Tanyan ecanun yelo* (You did well)!" Now we will go over to Pete Red Legs and borrow a horse and travois to haul them home."

It was only a few hundred yards over to Pete's place and he had several horses. We were all walking mighty tall when we hotfooted it into Pete's yard. He came out to meet us when his *sunka* (dog) started barking. Pete looked kinda tired and like he had just woke up, but when Unci told him we had two elk and wanted to borrow a horse and travois to haul them into camp, he sure came to life. His face woke up and he looked all excited and said, "We will take two horses and I will go too!"

"We will have plenty of meat now, and we will share it with our neighbors. That is the Indian way," said Unci. By the time Pete got the horses ready, there were several other men anxious to help, so we all headed out to get the elk. Unci went back to her house to get ready for the elk. Brave Bear and I didn't have to do any more with the elk, but there was sure a lot of busy women helping Unci that afternoon.

Mother had made arrangements for Aunt Mary and Uncle Joe to get me and Brave Bear back to school when they took Charlie and Arthur. They weren't late in getting to Unci's, but us boys sure weren't in any hurry to get back to school. Charlie and Arthur sat silently in the wagon while we gathered our things. We did go back with Vermilions, but before we left, Unci filled our pockets with many treats and hugged both Brave Bear and me. She kissed me right on the mouth! That took me by surprise. I had never been kissed on the mouth before. Well, it wasn't so bad, but only Unci could get away with that.

"I am so proud of you boys, and your great-grandfather Red Cloud would be proud of you too!" she said, as we were climbing onto the wagon. Then she added softly with very sad look on her face, "I am very old, and this may be the last time you will see me, t*ka* (but) I will be with you always. Just keep me in your heart, where it really counts."

"Oh, you will see us again, for sure. We will be back next summer!" I said, objecting to the very idea that Brave Bear and I would not be spending our summers with Unci forever.

School was really tough that year. It was very hard to talk just in English, and we got the soap treatment several times the first week back at school. That was the last time we saw Unci alive. She died the coming winter while we were in school.

Boys in school uniforms at Fort Yates Indian School about 1900. Photo by Frank Bennett Fiske used with permission of the State Historical Society of North Dakota.

CHAPTER 2

Winning the West River Country

Mother and Dad had moved our home again—this time we moved clear over to the west side of the reservation. Dad had said that the grass was better for cattle in the West River Country—that's what everybody called the land west of the Missouri. He was still hunting for the railroad crew, and game was easier to find in the tall grass and he could keep up with the new line, which was being laid a little at a time but was slowly moving west.

The government closed the garrison at Fort Yates that year and gave away many of the buildings. The houses and the stockade were made of big squared-off logs from the cottonwood trees that grew along the banks of the Missouri. Dad got to take an officer's house that he took apart in the fall; that winter, using two teams of horses, he and several friends hauled the logs back to our homestead near Thunder Hawk. He numbered each piece and then hauled them on a bobsled a few at a time along the frozen river that winter. The ice had to be hard froze and it could be cold up on the bobsled, but it was a lot easier using a bobsled than a wagon and the horses seemed to enjoy their winter labors. When spring came, he lengthened out the reach on the wagon and hauled the last few logs out to the

West River Country. He reconstructed the house in a small grove of trees, where there was already some chokecherries and buffalo berries growing. Several friends helped out with moving the logs but they had to make a lot of trips because they could only haul two or three logs at a time.

When the house was built back up, it was one of the best houses in the West River Country with two rooms downstairs and two rooms upstairs, a big porch out front, and lots of windows. Us kids got to help whitewash it inside and outside. We had some pictures on the walls; one was a really pretty colored photograph of Mother with a green blanket on her shoulders taken when she and Dad were first married. There was a buckskin quiver *(wáŋju)* that Mother's mother had decorated with beads when she was young hanging on the wall in the living room. Lots of people were coming through the country with too many things they didn't really need and not enough grain or horses or something they really needed. So Dad would trade them for things that Mother wanted for the house or her family. Mother smiled all day long when Dad traded a newly broke horse for a cast-iron cook stove. She was especially proud of the piano that Dad brought home for my sisters to play—some of them better than others—my baby sister Bess was the best, pounding out hymns that Mother sang for her and dance tunes that Dad played on his fiddle. Later at boarding school, she learned that music could be written down and read like words.

Dad's good friend from their younger days in the army, Jim Hourigan, was looking for greener pastures too, so he moved his family out west along with the folks. Jim was also married to an Indian woman, and he and Dad both liked to call themselves "Winners of the West." Dad liked that so much, he even made sure it was put on his tombstone.

Two states had been carved out of Dakota Territory, although the Standing Rock Reservation land was in both of them. Dad put our house on the North Dakota side of the line and Jim put his house a mile away on the South Dakota side. Others came into the area and town was beginning to grow up right along the new state line. Dad and Jim got to talking about what to call the settlement now that the there was train station and they needed a post office. Since the train tracks were in South Dakota, the town would be part of that state. Dad suggested that they call the town "Hourigantown."

Jim wouldn't have any of that, saying to Dad, "Why don't we just call it 'Gillandville.' Nobody could say that either." Then they got to being serious. Mother had just heard from her one of her cousins that old Chief Thunder Hawk had just died. Thunder Hawk was a well-respected local leader who had been a companion to Sitting Bull. He lived and camped with his people in the area all his life.

"Naming the town for Chief Thunder Hawk would keep his spirit alive," she said.

"Well, then, that's it. We should name our town to honor the old chief." Dad and Jim shook hands and that was it. The chief's name would live on in the town built on his old campgrounds.

There were other ranchers scattered along the Cedar River and Grand River. George Mentz had a good-size herd of cows about twenty-five miles east of us, on the north side of the Cedar River, and Jim Flying Horse had a bunch of cows on the Grand River about forty miles south and east of us. Although we sure didn't have many neighbors at first, it soon changed. Every year there were more settlers coming and looking for a place to get started, and Jim and Dad were always happy to show them around. Only Indians could settle on the reservation then, so until it was opened up for homesteading in 1909, the first families that stayed around our area were Indians or *breeds.* Whites called the children of mixed families like ours "half-breeds" or just "breeds," but Indians called a spade a spade. If we lived Indian, then we were considered Indian, and if we lived like the whites, we were thought of as white. If your heart was good, you were treated as friend in either case.

After Unci died, I stayed home all summer. Instead of hunting and gathering firewood, I got to drive a team on a mowing machine. Dad said that a good supply of hay was the difference between getting a herd through winter and starvation. The native grasses along the rivers grew belly deep to a horse in those days. Buffalo grass was best for grazing, but it was too short to make good hay. Needle grass and wild alfalfa with light purple flowers grew tall and made good hay, but western wheatgrass made the best winter feed for cattle and for horses too.

I can still remember being really excited the first time Dad told me I could mow and he showed me how everything worked—the mower sickle cut when the wheels turned, but if the wheels turned too fast it would plug the cutter bar, or break the sickle. There was a hay buncher behind the cutter bar and when it got full, you had to trip it with your right foot. Every hour I had to stop and oil the sickle head and other moving parts, and always unhook the tugs so when I was greasing the mower, or unplugging the cutter bar, the horses couldn't take off with the mower. They could still take off if I didn't keep a hand on the reins. If they did get away from me, they at least wouldn't drag the mower over me.

It seemed so simple. I soon learned it was very important to drive at the right speed. I started out just fine, Dad had already laid out a patch that he wanted cut, and all I had to do was drive the team and follow where the grass had already been cut and keep the mower close to the grass that wasn't cut. Well, easier said than done. The team was well broke, but they were always going too far right or too far left. About halfway around the field I hit a patch of sand grass—the mower made a racket, the sickle quit going, and the wheels were a sliding along. I was out in the cut area by the time I got the team stopped. "Dirty son of a skunk!" I swore under my breath. I did as Dad said, unhitched the tugs and started pulling grass from the plugged cutter bar.

I was still a pulling grass when Ben caught up with me. He was driving a mower too, and he had started ahead of me. He stopped and helped me get unplugged, then said, "Watch me, I'll show you how it is done." He just speeded up the horses when he hit that sand grass and went right on through. I learned the difference between grasses in a hurry!

By the time we were finished haying that summer, I could keep right up with Ben. We would cut a patch of five to ten acres, then we would rake it up in bunches, go out and haul it home right away, and stack it on the north side of the straw-roofed shed. The shed was made of ash poles set in the ground, with three planks nailed to the poles about three feet apart, parallel to the ground, then boards nailed to the planks, in an upright fashion. Longer poles were set upright down the center of the shed, and a center ridge was nailed to them. Cottonwood poles were peeled and nailed from the center ridge to the walls, and boards were nailed to the cottonwood poles crossways leaving a foot gap between the boards, and then two or three feet of straw was placed over the boards.

We didn't usually have straw so we used hay on the roof of the shed. We had to pitch the hay onto the hayrack and me and Ted would tramp it in the rack. Ben and Dad would pitch the hay up to us, then we pulled it off with the team, using a system we figured out for ourselves. We spread two ropes on the bottom of the hayrack, about four feet apart, and tied them to a ring. We hooked the ring on the center upright of the hayrack before we started pitching the hay in. Next we would back up to the end of the stack and anchor the ends of the ropes hanging off the back of the hayrack to long ropes tied to the bottom of a post way out front. Then we hooked another rope over the top of the hayrack to the ring in front and tied the other end of that rope to a doubletree hooked to the team facing the opposite direction from the hayrack. When we drove the team ahead, the hay in the rack would come a rolling along, and we could roll hay up in a stack forty feet high if we wanted to.

Dad always wanted the haystack, high, wide, and long. After we got well over a hundred ton of hay stacked around the barn, we would rake the hay to the middle of the cut, and pitch it into a pile. Again, me and Ted had the job of leveling it off, tramping it, and rounding off the top so rain would run off. Then us boys had to put a fence around the haystack, and Dad would hitch a team onto the plow and plow a few furrows around the haystack fence. Dad worried about a fire getting started and that was his precaution. Also some of those big cattle outfits' longhorn steers was always drifting by, and if the hay wasn't fenced in, those steers would just wreck a haystack in nothing flat.

Ben didn't have to go to school anymore but Ted and I still had to go. We were closer to Mandan now and there was an Indian school there, so off we went to Mandan. Mother would have let us miss school some, but Dad was a firm believer in a good education, so he always managed to have time to take us, or he made sure we got there by some means. The school at Mandan was a lot like the one at Fort Pierre. There were mostly different kids going there, but we knew quite a few of them too, including some of our Vermillion cousins. There was also Goodreaus, McLaughlins, Black Hoops, Two Bears, Keeps Eagles, and Bringsums that we knew from living over near the Porcupine settlement, and we soon got acquainted with some from the Fort Yates area too.

In the wintertime, some of the boys from Fort Yates would skate home on the frozen Missouri River, spend a weekend at home, and then skate back to the school. A few times Ted and I skated along. Charlie and Arthur really skated fast and could be at their house in two or three hours. Since our Granddad and Grandmother McEldery lived at Fort Yates, Ted and I usually stayed with them. It was crowded at Aunt Mary's and I didn't like having to put up with Charlie and Arthur always skulking around.

Skating was a little dangerous; there was always air pockets where the ice was real thin. Sometimes the water would even be open for ten to forty feet, and if you were going fast you couldn't stop, so you just had to jump the water and hope you hit ice that would hold you up. I remember a time when the ice broke under one skate, but the other one held, so I used that one and went on along. But my last year at the Mandan school, they stopped letting anyone skate down the river because two boys that had headed home didn't show up anywhere. It was suspected that they tried jumping an open spot in the river and didn't jump far enough and went under the ice. They may have just ran away too, so no one looked hard to find them. At any rate, that extracurricular activity came to a stop.

At last, I graduated from the eighth grade. No more school for me! But I was going home feeling really down in the mouth. Ted had died a few months back and it was going to be lonesome at home without him—like losing your shadow. Dad made sure I didn't have time to dwell a lot about Ted dying. He had built up a big cattle herd and there was more work to do than we seemed to be able to get done in two days, but we were always trying to get it done in one.

A lot of people were traveling through the area now, and Dad was always selling them a fresh team or a saddle horse, and there was getting to be quite a few people settling in the area. We had been wintering our cattle a few miles north of Thunder Hawk Creek on the Cedar River, but there were too many others moving into that area now: besides our Vermilion and Powers relatives, Hodgkinsons, Bensons, and Wagners all ran cattle in that area. The area around the new town of Thunder Hawk was getting taken up by all the settlers, and there was good grass and better shelter for the cattle down on the Grand River.

Benjamin Gilland with grandson, Jimmy Gayton about 1903.

Elizabeth Gilland holding her youngest daughter Elizabeth with Annie Gilland Gayton standing about 1896.

After we were done haying at home, Dad sent me down to the Grand River about twenty miles south to help Ben put up hay and to break some horses. There was still a lot of longhorn steers mixed in with our cows so Ben and I rode for over a week kicking them south and east. Those longhorns were mean as billy ol' hell. They weren't supposed to be on reservation land anymore grazing for free, but it took the big cattle companies a few years after their leases was up to round up all their cattle.

We were not too far away from where old Chief Thunder Hawk was buried with his family a ways back from a big horseshoe bend in the Grand River. A couple of years ago, about the time of the new century, a cyclone swept through the area and made a new hill on the north bank out of the dirt from the river bottomland and about twenty-five of the people camped there. Nobody knows for sure how many because they were never found again. If you looked up from the river, you could see the in cliffs above the river where the cyclone had left stripes of lighter-colored soil that didn't look like the rest of the riverbanks. It was the same light brown as the river bottomland, and smooth river rocks, dark rock chips, and little stones stuck out all over.

That storm caught everyone by surprise as they thought that being camped down below the cliffs on the riverbanks would given them shelter. But those cyclone winds come out of nowhere. Some said they could still find bits and pieces of tepees, beadwork, knives, and other things scattered as far away as Black Horse Butte. Felix Fly told me his grandfather told him that they found Nick Blanket hanging from a tree with his long braids all twisted around the branches. His hat was driven right into the truck of a cottonwood tree. There was nothing left of his shirt except the collar and cuffs and nothing left of his pants but the waistband and pockets. A lot of people who died were never found so the area was kind of a *wáŋǧi* (ghost) place and the tribe never camped there after that storm. I thought that hill must be a graveyard and we always stayed a respectful distance away from that place. The cattle wouldn't go near that hill and the horses shied away too, making our job a little easier.

Dad and Ben had already built a camp on the other side of the river and Ben had wintered there last year and broke a bunch of horses. Mother was worried Ben was developing a liking for the spirit waters, and Dad figured getting him away from the source and giving him plenty to do would keep him from becoming a drunk. Brave Bear had ran away from that Indian school over at Fort Pierre and stayed with Ben most of the past winter helping him with the horses. But he got restless and just left awhile before I had gotten home so I didn't get to see him. Ben said that Brave Bear had told him that he was afraid someone might find him if he stayed any longer and he sure wasn't going back to that school.

Altogether, we had about four hundred fifty head of cattle to get through the winter along the Grand, and Dad had near about one hundred head up Thunder Hawk way to keep him occupied. We pushed our cows up on Thunder Hawk Creek, where there was open water and the grass was real good. Ben figured, if we started the cows along the creek, we could work them closer to the home camp as winter progressed, as it was only about five miles away. Dad had sorted off the older cows and bulls and would winter them up at Thunder Hawk, so we just had yearlings and younger cows, and two-year-old and three-year-old steers to worry about. We could open water for the cattle with the horses we were breaking, and if the winter got bad, we could hook up a team and feed the cattle hay. We had stacked hay in several places close to our camp, so we were set for all winter.

CHAPTER 3

Black Horse Butte Camp

It was already the first part of November and we were well into breaking horses when it started snowing, only a few inches, but in a couple of days it snowed some more, and this pattern kept up. By Christmastime we had twenty inches of snow and the cattle were having a hard time grazing, so we had to move them down on the river about two miles from where they were. The snow was too deep to try hauling anything on wagon wheels. Dad had left us a couple of bobsleds—these had two sets of sled runners with a tongue and bolster on the front one and a reach back to the second runner with a bolster on it—so we put the hayracks on them and hauled hay out to the cattle every day.

We skipped the cattle on Christmas day because Mother always wanted all her family home for Christmas. Early in the afternoon of Christmas Eve, we hooked up a team to a jumper sled—a sled with a single set of runners—and made it to Thunder Hawk after dark. My older sisters Sadie and Annie didn't make it because there was just too much snow. They were both married now: Sadie had married an Indian rancher by the name of Ben Defender and they lived over south of Fort Yates, and Annie married Charlie Gayton and lived over about ten miles west of Fort Yates.

We ate Mother's delicious dinner on Christmas day and left the table as soon as we'd had our fill of mincemeat pie to hitch up the jumper sled so we could get back to winter camp that night. We woke up early to heavy snowfall, so we made tracks and loaded up the bobsled with hay and headed over to the cattle. There was only about two hundred head to be found, so we fed the ones that were there and hightailed it back to camp. The next day it was snowing again. We drove up to the cattle and they all started to bunch around us, so we headed back down river 'til we were a mile or so from camp and then we pitched off the hay, and opened water. Every day the cattle were waiting for us and seemed to be getting hungrier, so we had to feed more hay. Now we were hauling three loads of hay a day and the cattle weren't grazing any.

Every day we talked about going to look for the missing cattle—we were short more than two hundred head, but there just wasn't enough time in the day to go look for any more cattle and we had about as many as we could keep up with anyway. We didn't get a break in the weather until the first part of March, when it got warm enough to thaw some and the cattle went to grazing on the ridges and we didn't have to feed so much. We got done early enough in the afternoon to saddle up a couple of horses and go looking for the missing cattle. I thought, they'll all be dead by now, but Ben insisted that we find them. We rode back up the river to where we had last seen cattle, then went south a couple of miles, and there were the cattle. They had gotten into some rough country and there was a big spring with running water. The cattle were just a grazing along and they looked in better shape than the ones we had been feeding.

"Looks like we should have pushed all the cattle out this way. Sure could of saved a lot of hay," Ben said. We just left the cattle that were out in the breaks where they were and headed back to camp.

It wasn't long before the snow was a melting quite a bit and there was grass sticking up in a lot of places, and the cattle were losing interest in hay, so we didn't have to feed much. One day Ben saddled up and as he swung into the saddle, said with a determined look, "I think you can handle things here at camp for a day. I'm going to ride over west to that settlement just on the other side of the reservation, and see if they made it through the winter."

This took me by surprise. We had been expecting Dad to show up with supplies just about any day. Ben was pretty tough, but he still had plenty of respect for Dad. I had witnessed a few fights he had been in over at that Indian school, out behind the barn, and he was quick on his feet and dang good with his dukes. Once two big boys came at him at the same time, and he had them both sitting on their butts on the ground with blood running out of their faces, and they didn't want any more fight. It was Dad who had taught us boys how to defend ourselves, and with boxing gloves on, Ben was no match for him, but respect would keep him from trying the old man, anyway.

Ben must have read my thoughts and he came back with, "If Dad shows up, just tell him I went over to get some supplies," and he rode off west on a fast trot.

Two days went by and no Ben, then three, and the fourth day, I got to thinking I'd better go looking for him, but I had over twenty broke horses to feed in the corral and just couldn't go off and leave them. So I got the idea I would take all the horses up to Dad and then go look for Ben. I headed the horses north—the ice wasn't out of the river yet but it would be shortly with all the thawing we had been having. I was a little over halfway home with the horses when, lo and behold, here came Dad along in a buggy. I told him what I was up to and that I was a little worried about Ben not getting back.

"Son, you just take them horses on home and jump on a fresh horse and get on back across the river before that ice goes out," he said. It was like he was squashing the words out between his teeth. The buggy wheels were a spinning a lot faster now than when I met him a coming down the trail, and he headed right for that Seim's settlement. Lou Seim had built a general store with a bunkhouse and pool hall over west of the reservation where the north and south forks of the Grand River come together, right about fifteen miles west of the our winter camp in the timber allotments.

When I got home, I ran to the house and Mother fixed me a quick meal of warmed-up biscuits and stew, and I was off for camp again. I made it back and the ice was still holding together but there was water on top of the ice so it was about to go out. After I fixed supper, I washed up the dishes and tidied up a little, lit a kerosene lamp, and was deep in reading a book, when I heard someone riding in. Ben came in, looking about like death warmed over, and just went right to his bed and plopped down on it, and I think he was snoring in less than a minute. The next morning, Ben said he had gotten in with some of those wranglers from the L-7 outfit and they just had to celebrate getting through the winter, but Dad had came along and that abruptly ended their party.

The cattle were grazing mostly now but we still fed a little hay to them. The snow was leaving, and it was getting hard to keep the sled on snow; it pulled plenty hard on bare ground so we switched and put the wagon wheels back under the hayracks. Changing the racks wasn't much of a job with two people, but alone it would be a different story. We had cut five big cottonwood logs about four foot long and we used a pole for a pry bar. By putting the pry bar over one of the cut-off logs standing on end we pried up one corner of the rack and put another cut-off log under that corner while the other person held the corner up with the pry bar. We did that with all the corners, then we pulled the sled out from under the rack and pulled the wagon wheels under the rack and reversed our procedure.

After we fed the cattle, Ben said, "Dad wants us to break another bunch of horses. We'd better head down around Black Horse Butte and bring in some of our horses that were wintering there." We hoped they were, anyhow. We were soon in the saddle and looking for horses. It was only about seven miles from camp, but the horses could be anywhere! We rode up to the bottom of the butte and hadn't seen a horse, but there were signs of horses being in the area. So we rode on up to the top, and then we could see horses in little bunches scattered along from a little ways west of the butte to way over next to the reservation line—about seven miles. Black Horse Butte was the highest hill in that country and you could see a long ways from up there. We also seen five riders heading our way and they were only about two miles away. Ben said that it must be some of the L-7 or the Turkey Track cowboys out looking for strays.

Back in about 1877 when the reservations were formed, the government hired a crew to put a four-wire fence around the reservation to help keep the Indian renegades from leaving and to keep white renegades from slipping guns and whiskey to the natives on the reservation. The reservation was still fenced all around the boundary and there was a border patrol riding along the border about twice a week, but you never knew what day you might see them. No one could come onto the reservation without first getting a permission slip from the Agency over at Fort Yates, and anybody caught on the reservation without that permission slip was promptly escorted right over to the Agency, so not many white people ventured over on the reservation. The big cattle outfits' riders all carried slips, and us breeds and Indians had a registration card to prove we were Indians. There wasn't a charge for the permission slips, but it was more than a hundred miles to Fort Yates. I never heard of anyone ever being refused a slip, but there was a $25 fine for being caught without one, and the border police escorted anybody caught anywhere without one over to the Agency to pay up.

Anyway, Ben said that we might as well head all the horses west and bunch them over there and try to cut out twenty head of the ones we have to get broke. We headed the horses west, but we had only traveled a mile or so when suddenly there were five riders coming at us from the north side, and they were coming right at us and they weren't just a meandering along. It was the Duncan clan—Henry Duncan's kids: Charles Jr., Lora, Tom, Bill, and Kittie. They all rode up smiling and I think I might have brightened up a little too, especially when I seen Kittie. She was a really pretty girl, about my age, and she could ride horse like the wind. Both girls were dressed in trousers and wide hats much like their brothers, but they sure looked a lot better in them.

We all said our hi's, then Charles and Ben did the talking.

Charles said that their dad had sent them out to find their horses. The fence must have gotten down somewhere and their horses had gotten all mixed with ours. We all knew that the Duncans had been turning their horses, and sometimes cattle too, over on the reservation, but it didn't matter to Ben and me. There was a lot of grass and it was up to the Agency to catch them if they didn't like it. Ben told of our plan to bunch the horses on the west line just east of the ridge called Hogback Ridge. Charles said, "Let's get at it then. We can sort our horses off over there too, and kick them through the gate on that side and head them on home." The Hogback was only a couple of miles south of the Duncan headquarters.

We were soon holding over a hundred horses bunched on the reservation line. Ben and Charles did most of the sorting—they just brought out the younger horses that they knew weren't broke. The Duncans' young horses got pushed through the gate and Tom was out there a heading them north and holding them. Bill was watching the gate and our horses were headed north and I held them from running back to the bunch. We had twenty-five horses sorted our way and the Duncans had about as many when Ben said, "Well, that is enough for us, so we better just head them for home while we still have light." With the very serious look his face took on when he was kidding, Ben said, "Charles, we can come back tomorrow and help you get the rest of your horses sorted off if you want."

"We have the ones we want to get to riding anyway, but we'll be back real soon and get the rest of our horses," Charles said, matching Ben's look with a determined sound to his voice. I thought, that sounds like double-talk to me. I really doubt if they ever get their horses off the reservation the rest of the summer. Charles said, "Bill, why don't you go help Tom with our horses and shut the gate, and the girls and I'll head the other horses south and get them out of the way for the Gilland boys."

We all waved and Charles and the girls whisked the herd of horses south in a flash, and in nothing flat they were gone plumb out of sight. Ben and I headed northeast with the little bunch we had and were not wasting any time—we had about eight miles to go and some dang rough country to cross, and the sun was already getting about halfway low in the west.

We were just crossing what we called Ben's Creek, about a mile from camp, when two riders came up behind us. Right away, I could see it was Kittie and Lora. They came a riding up and Lora said, with a big smile, "Charles sent us to help you boys get your horses though all that rough country, and he said if it got dark, we would just have to stay at your camp for the night." Ben sat there looking kind a dumb with his mouth open, but he didn't seem to find any words to say, and I was totally dumbfounded. I thought, girls staying with us! Where will we sleep them? We left the house a mess, what will they think?

Kittie was all smiles too, "Oh don't worry, we can manage, and if you don't have extra beds, we can even sleep on the floor. Let's get these horses in your corral before it gets so dark we can't find the corral!" It didn't take long to corral the horses and get ours fed and unsaddled. The girls tied their horses in the shed and we all headed for the house. Lora took charge right away of fixing something to eat and she had Ben a showing her where everything was. I helped Kittie get dishes on the table and after we had eaten, I helped her wash the dishes. Lora went to tidying up the house and Ben got out some extra bedding and made up a couple of bedrolls on the floor.

"It's too early to just go to bed. Do you boys know how to play cards?" Lora asked. Ben and I had played cards a lot. Ben went over to the cabinet and brought out a deck of cards and handed them to Lora. We all sat back around the table and Lora dealt out the cards. "Let's make it seven-card stud. We didn't bring any money so we'll just have to play for our clothes," she said while squashing her hat down on her head. "Is that OK with you boys?" This about flabbergasted me! I had played a little poker, but never for clothes, and never with women.

Ben looked more than a little surprised too, but he spoke up, "Sure, why not." So the game began. The girls weren't very good players and Lora lost her hat right away. They lost their boots and socks and trousers first, and Ben lost his shirt and boots, and I lost my boots and neck scarf, then Lora lost her shirt. She was really pretty under that shirt, but I lost my concentration on playing and lost my shirt too. Then Kittie lost her shirt and Lora lost her camisole. I hadn't seen many girls without clothes on before (just my sisters sometimes when they were taking baths behind the stove), but I was all eyes now and Kittie looked like she was just as full in the chest as her sister, but she still had on a camisole.

Lora said, "I'm not going to play 'til I lose everything (she still had her bloomers), and she got up and jumped into Ben's bed.

That ended our game, but everyone was about out of clothes anyway. It was quite a game and one I wouldn't soon forget! I just crawled under a blanket on the floor and Kittie took my bed, and Ben blew out the light, and laid down someplace.

In a little while, there was a whisper in my ear, "Come on over to your bed. We can just sleep together in your bed, and we don't have to do anything but sleep." I woke up with the sun a shining in my face and my long johns were gone, and so was Kittie. Kittie and Lora were both up and firing up the stove and were getting breakfast a cooking. Kittie seen I was awake and gave me a big grin, "Are you going to get dressed for breakfast or are you coming to the table naked?" Didn't take me long to shinny into my clothes in plenty of time for breakfast.

Right after breakfast, the girls saddled up and headed home, but Kittie gave me a big hug and a long kiss before she swung up into her saddle. I wasn't watching but I think Lora might have given Ben a peck or two too. We were in love (or at least puppy love). Before the girls left, they had invited us to a party at their house next Saturday night, and, of course, we agreed we would come.

The Duncans had invited everyone in the whole area to their party. Ben and I were right on time, and Kittie and Lora came out to greet us and I got a quick kiss from Kittie. She was smiling when she said, "I have to be proper in public, you know!" She took my arm and was shortly introducing me to all the ones that I didn't know and then supper was ready. There was a big meal, and then there would be a dance. The Duncan house was big—about thirty feet wide and at least sixty feet long with a big upstairs. The kitchen and dining room were all in one, and with all the furniture moved outside there was quite a bit of room for dancing. There was one big bedroom at the far end of the house and up the stairs six bedrooms. But I didn't plan to stay all night, and with all the people there, the house would surely be fully occupied.

The dance started, but I had never danced in my life (except for Indian dancing and that was a whole lot different kind of dancing). I was sure watching other people dance; Ben and Lora were dancing good, and a lot of others. Roy Groat had the dance with Kittie, then there was Jake Wiener dancing with her, and next was Tom Powers, and then George Minges. It looked like I was just going to get to watch, but I couldn't dance anyway. I was just standing there a minding my own business when there was a hand tapping me on the arm. I turned to look see who it was and there was Mrs. Duncan, all smiles and her eyes just sparkled. She said, "Young man, it's about time you were a learning to dance. Come along and I'll teach you!" They were playing a slow two-step and she told me, "Just follow my lead. It's two steps one way, then one back the other and you just step in time with the music." I did as she said and managed to get through that dance.

Kittie came along then and swung me away from her mother saying, "My turn," and we started shuffling along with the music. I was getting the hang of it and could even turn slowly, when the musicians stopped and took a break.

Ben grabbed my arm and said, "Let's go outside and check the stars!" I knew something was up—Ben wasn't interested at looking at the stars. We got outside and he handed me a flask saying, "Here have a drink. It'll limber you up so you can dance better!" I hadn't ever taken a drink of whiskey, but I had tasted it a few times. I took a big drink, and in a minute, old Charley Duncan handed me a bottle, too. I couldn't be rude to him by not having a drink with him so I took a drink. Most of the men that were inside dancing were now outside and about all of them had a bottle and they weren't Scotch with their bottles. I took quite a few drinks from different ones. When the music started playing again, and most went back inside, I wasn't feeling so good. Felt like I might even heave, so I took a stroll far out behind the shed, and sure enough I did have to heave and I was really sick. I had a hell of a time just trying to walk, so I just sat down and leaned up against a haystack and rested my eyes.

The sun was just coming up and I was still leaning against that haystack, and did I have a headache. I looked around and could see that most of the crowd had already left so I thought, that is probably the best solution for me too. I found my horse and got saddled and went a heading home, and hoped no one was up yet to see me. Ben's horse was still in the corral so I figured he must have stayed somewhere around there too, but I didn't see him and I sure didn't feel like looking for him. I was thinking, I wonder what Kittie will think of me now. She will think I'm just a drunk! That dang Ben and his spirit waters. It was about six miles back to camp and my horse went a bouncing along, I hadn't noticed before just how rough a riding horse he was. But he finally bounced himself home, and I turned him loose and headed to the house and just flopped down on my bed. Now I knew what Ben felt like when he had came home and just hit the bed asleep!

It was midafternoon when I heard Ben come a stomping in. He was in good spirits and just a grinning every time he looked my way. He said, "You missed a lot of dancing by going home so early." I got up and drank about a half gallon of water and was feeling a little better.

About then Dad walked in. "Looks like you boys are just a laying around, but your vacation is over. I have a lot of work lined up to get done right away," he said. Then he told us, "There is talk of the Agency opening up the reservation for homesteading and each of us can file on a homestead too. When they open up the land, we just as well get squatted on the quarters of land we want and get some buildings put up." The government had already given each enrolled member of the tribe a quarter section of land, and mother got a half section. Altogether, we had taken seven quarters of land just on the north side of Thunder Hawk. So we took a buggy ride looking for land. We looked a lot, and finally decided to take the three-quarter sections just south of the river from where we had wintered some of the cattle.

The rest of the summer was busy—we were haying when we could, and if it rained, we were cutting or hauling logs for our log houses. When the government did open the reservation for homesteading in 1909, we were about the first in line to stake a claim, and we were already set up with a log house on each quarter. Dad had taken the first quarter south of the river, I took the second one, and Ben took the quarter on the south side of mine. We had to live on our claims at least six months a year, but we still had cattle running at large and there was a lot of land yet to be homesteaded so, we didn't change the operation all that much. Ben and I moved back to the camp in our timber allotments, and Dad went back to

Thunder Hawk for the winter. But now we were getting a lot of neighbors and there was a community just east a ways where we could get supplies. Dad wasn't much on paying us a lot of wages, but he gave us cattle and horses for our wages, so Ben and I were getting started in the cattle business.

Rounding up cattle on the open range about 1905. Photo by Frank Bennett Fiske used with permission of the State Historical Society of North Dakota.

CHAPTER 4

Lela Waste, Mato Ohitika (Good Day, Brave Bear)

Looked like a storm brewing. It was getting cloudy in the west and *lila tate* (very windy). I would be glad to get my newly bought herd of Aberdeen Angus home. A rider had been trailing behind most of the afternoon but I hadn't seen him for a while. Maybe he was just a drunk cowboy heading home after a wild weekend in Evarts. I get a little nervous when someone pokes along behind me and I don't know his intensions. Cottonwood Creek was just ahead. I figured to make it there with the cows and spread out my bedroll up there for the night. Ben and my little brother Abe would be along in the morning to help me get my herd home from the "Strip."

The six-mile wide stretch of land known as the Strip was fenced on both sides with gates every few miles all the way across the Standing Rock Reservation from the Missouri River on the east side to Thunder Hawk on the west side. The Milwaukee Railroad, the white ranchers, and the Indian agencies at Standing Rock and Cheyenne River all agreed that the Strip could be used by any cattlemen free of charge—but no sheep were allowed. The white ranchers who grazed their cattle on the reservations used it to get their cattle to the grazing lands, and Indian ranchers used it to move their cattle to and from the railhead at the town of Evarts on the Missouri.

Whoa, horse! I knew someone was coming up behind me before I even turned in the saddle by the way my horse started acting. I hoped it wasn't trouble looking me in the eye as I turned and looked over my shoulder with my hand on my Colt .38. I'd done a lot of practicing shooting gophers from a running horse, but I hoped I wouldn't have to use it. Ever since they opened up the reservation for homesteading, and stopped patrolling the border, there had been a lot of rustling in the area.

"Hey! Wanbli Luta."

I knew that voice and tall frame in the saddle even before he got close enough for me to see his face under the wide brim of his black hat.

"*Mato Ohitika*!" I said, "*Waste, Lela Waste* (Good day, very good day). *Toniktuka hwo?* (How are you?)"

He rode up with his hand out. We shook hands heartily—his grip was like iron. We sat on our horses a few minutes taking in how the years had changed each of us since Indian school. Brave Bear's high-crowned Stetson was decorated with a narrow beaded band (no doubt the work of a woman's hand) and he had on a pair of good boots. His gear hadn't seen too much wear, so I knew he must be doing pretty well. He'd grown an inch or two taller than me. I'd kept my hair short since Indian school, and I seen that Brave Bear had too. Mine had a more of a glint of golden red in it, but we both had the same not quite black, not quite brown hair. Mother said my slate-blue eyes came from the Gilland side so I guess he probably got his golden eyes from his white father. Both of use had eyes squinted up from looking at the long distance, though Brave Bear's had a wary look about them that I didn't think mine had yet taken on. I thought my nose was a little sharper and my chin more set than his, but he had always had a deep cleft in his chin, now grown deeper. I had to admit that he had gotten handsome, and I bet the girls noticed too.

Robert Gilland (Red Eagle) about 1908.

"Well, how you been, my friend?" Brave Bear said with a grin as big as the sky. We dismounted and headed for an old log to perch on. "It's been quite awhile, since we were boys at that Indian School in Fort Pierre."

I told him I went back to Thunder Hawk after I graduated from the eighth grade and about how I'd been helping my dad and brothers work cattle and break horses. "Last winter Ben and I broke ten teams and about twenty-five saddle horses. Dad sells them horses at Thunder Hawk just as fast as we get them up there, and for good money, at least $300 a team. He sold a really well-matched team just before I left the other day for $1,400. Ben and I had camped all winter over on the Grand River on our timber lots. It's a good sheltered place in the winter but them damnable mosquitoes in the summer just about drove us crazy, so we quit camp and moved back to our homesteads just last week." I went on to tell him that I left two days ago to go over to Aberdeen and bring back this herd of Angus.

"I was glad to get away from broncs for a while. Rode horse to Evarts and took the train to Aberdeen and brought the cows back to Evarts by train, and now you've caught up with me taking them home. I had to get the money from Dad to buy these black hides. He doesn't want anything to do with them; he said they are solely my venture."

Dad had always made money with Red Durhams, and I doubt he will ever change breeds in his lifetime. I thought briefly back to when he topped the market at Chicago with his Durham steers in 1897—he got $16 a head, when most were only bringing $14. That year he splurged and brought back a brand new 12-gauge shotgun to shoot ducks with. There was an old slough over west of Thunder Hawk about ten miles and we shot ducks over there lots of times.

"Ben wants to get him some Hereford bulls, and then we will cross our cattle back and forth." I went on telling him about our ranching plans. "Ben and I filed on homesteads just south of the Grand River, about twenty miles northwest of here. Dad has a homestead there too, but spends most of his time with Mother at Thunder Hawk. We still run cattle and horses from Black Horse Butte to Thunder Hawk, along with several other Indian ranchers and the L-7.

"There used to be other big cattle companies running cattle on the reservation too, besides Ed Lemmon's L-7 outfit, but they were pretty much wiped out by the bad winters of 1898–99 and then last year. We always helped round up the cattle on the reservation then sorted out each owner's cattle for shipping. We still help the L-7 outfit, but the Matador, Hat, and the others are gone. Turkey Track runs cattle up north on the Cedar River and east, clear to Fort Yates, but them white homesteaders are fast taking up a lot of range and putting up fences and trying to turn the ground wrong side up."

I rattled on, telling him how confused homesteaders from back east can be. "As fast as them homesteaders get settled, they all have to burn up their boxes and garbage, and they have started grass fires, some really bad ones. Last summer I got caught in the front of one, thought for a little while I might get burned too, but I quick lit a fire and got in the burned-off spot. That fire came at me forty miles an hour and flames rolling ahead of it thirty feet in the air.

When it got to the Grand River it just shot up the trees on one side and over to the tops on the other side and back down to the ground and all the way to the Missouri River. A herd of antelope came a running into the burn with me and they crowded so close to me I could reach out and touch them."

When I finally realized how I'd been talking his ears off, I gulped hard, grinned at myself, and said to Brave Bear, "Toniktuka hwo?"

He laughed and said, "Oh, I'm as fine as *gnaska hin* (frog hair)! I've covered a lot of territory since I quit that Indian school. Spent some time in the Black Hills and worked with a Wild West show for a while, but they wanted me to go to Europe, so I quit. It was an easy job—I just had to ride around in a breechcloth and shoot balloons. I got pretty good at gambling too, but they said I cheated and threw me in jail. But I hadn't cheated. When I got out of jail, I came back to the reservation and have been breaking horses for different ones, and doing odd jobs to make spending money."

"Why didn't you catch up this afternoon and help me trail these cattle?" I asked, a little puzzled.

"Ah, Bob," he said like he was defending his actions, "I wasn't sure it was you for quite a while and I have to be kinda careful as to who I ride up to these days. Wanted man, you know—they put a price on my head over at Fort Yates awhile back. The law said I wiped out some homesteader and stole his horse. I did shoot him and I did take his horse, but it was self-defense. My horse came up lame so I stopped at his place and traded him my horse and gave him fifty bucks to boot. Then, just as I was about to get on his horse, he came at me with a pitchfork. I swung around and shot him but another three feet and I would have had pitchfork tines coming out my belly. I suppose he seen I had quite a bit of money in my pouch when I gave him the $50 and he must have figured to stab me and take all my money.

"Didn't figure the law would believe me anyway. They never have yet, so I just threw him down a well he was digging and worked half the night filling it in. I doubt anyone will ever find him but they still put out a reward, not much of a reward, only

$100, but enough to make a lot of do-gooders want to take me in. I think someone must have seen me riding his horse and the law thinks they can charge me with horse theft at the Fort. He must have had some influential relatives back somewhere. I don't think there's any way they can charge me with that crime, but I'm not going to turn myself in to find out. I did that once back a couple of years ago and they locked me up for a year for something I didn't even do. No, don't ever trust the law! Every time I have, I get time in jail.

"Anyway, as soon as I got over to Bob Bobtail Blue Bear's, I bought a good horse from him and just turned that old homesteader's nag lose. There's been other stories about me too—some are about half true—and some are just some asshole's imagination. That's why I have to be a little cautious, ya know. I believe some would shoot me just to get the reward if they have half a chance, but they won't get it if I keep my wits about me.

"I've made a lot of friends since we were boys at that damned Indian school over at Fort Pierre, but I've made a few enemies too. Remember when we got caught talking 'injun,' as they called it, and Sister Mary put soap in our mouths and we had to wash out our mouths? We got caught talking with our hands too and that old heifer made us put our hands on the desk and she whacked them with a ruler. Them were memorable days indeed! I ran away and never went back, but you must have persevered, and got through it."

"Things like that are hard to forget!" I said.

"I kinda got back at that old Sister Mary last summer," he said, with a sheepish grin on his face. "Her and two other nuns were heading up the trail to Bullhead in an old buggy. She recognized me right away and tried acting like an old lost friend, but I'd too many bad memories with her at that school, so her friendly attitude didn't set well with me. I didn't say anything 'til I got alongside their buggy, then I pulled up my Colt and said to them: 'The last one of you old sisters standing in that buggy with clothes on is going to get shot and the first one undressed will get to have sex.' Sister Mary was the first to strip naked but it was a close race. They were so damned ugly naked I decided I didn't hate my *shay* (penis) that much, so I just fired in the air and their horses bolted and all three of them tumbled off the back end of that buggy. It was quite a sight—couldn't help but laugh a little. I just tipped my hat and galloped on down the trail for quite a ways.

"They wandered into Ward's place still bare-ass naked and old Jake Ward went and gathered up their team and buggy and clothes and they got back on up to Bullhead. Suppose they had to go save all those sinners up there. Mrs. Ward sure scolded me and called me a scallywag when I stopped by their place the other day. What's a scallywag, anyway?"

"I don't know." I said kind of doubtful, "Maybe it is a *hogleglega tankal un mni* (grass pike fish out of water)." I had to laugh hard at the picture of Sister Mary running naked through the tall grass, but I thought maybe Brave Bear's punishment for the nuns was little harsh. I'd have settled for watching that old Heca wash her mouth out with some of that soap of hers every time she said a word that wasn't *injun.*

"It's good to see you again!" Brave Bear said. "I had heard you were down on the Rosebud Reservation."

I told him that I hadn't been over at Rosebud since Unci died. I stayed at home over the summers and had to ride a lot and herd cattle. That's when I decided to get good at shooting my pistol. One day back when I was about twelve, I was out riding around the cattle. I heard a cow bawling over in a little draw. I rode my pony (Dad had gotten me a small horse so I could get on easier) right over there, and there were about a dozen wolves around her, but the wolves already had her hamstrung and were eating on her back-end and had it all ate out. I rode at them a shooting and emptied my pistol at them and only got two and maybe wounded a couple more. Then I reloaded my pistol and shot the cow. I decided then that I was going to do a lot of practicing, so next time I wouldn't miss so much!

"I just got us invited to supper over at Louie Archambault's," Brave Bear confessed. "That's where I went instead of catching up to you. Let's get to going. *Hiyu w* (come on). We can talk on the way."

"*Tohan tehan ti hwo* (How far away does he live)?" I asked.

"It's only two or three miles over there," Brave Bear said, "and your herd will be OK here on the Strip tonight; it's fenced on both sides and I'll help you gather them in the morning. Old Louie has a haystack to sleep in. Looks like rain anyway, and it will be a lot warmer there than out here under a tree, guaranteed!"

I'd never been to Archambault's place, but a hot meal and a warm place to sleep sure sounded good. Louie put his haystack a few feet from his straw shed then laid poles parallel across from the hay to the top of his shed. Then he put more hay over the poles and closed in the west end with hay so he could feed his horses in the wintertime through windows in his shed without the wind blowing his hay away. "It does look like a good place to roll out bedrolls and it'll be dry. *Magaju ekta hanyetu* (Might rain tonight)!" I replied.

The place was well located in a horseshoe bend of a wooded draw on Louie's Creek. Lamps were lit in the house and it was getting near dark outside as we rode into the yard. "Let's eat first," Brave Bear said as he swung off his old pony and tied his reins to a corral rail. I did the same and we headed for the house.

A middle-aged Lakota gent came to the door. He was tall and big all over—a handsome fellow for his age. He greeted Brave Bear with a handshake and a slap on the shoulder, then gave me a cold look, and said, "*Nituwe hwo* (To whom am I speaking)? This must be that friend you spoke of earlier, Wanbli Luta?"

Brave Bear said, "Sure is, and a better friend you'll never find. He's a half-breed too—whites call him Bob Gilland." Louie's expression mellowed like softened butter now, and he shook my hand and said to come on in, that the missus has supper on. It was a big house for an "injun shack," but there was a raft of kids from a toddler on up to some twenty or so years old. There was two extra plates at the table, and the kids were already seated.

Louie's wife came around from behind the table and shook hands. "I'm Maria. Welcome to our home, please sit down." She told us all the kids' names as we were sitting down. Alice and Lizzy were the oldest, then Louie Jr., and Phoebe was the youngest and a real cutie. All the girls were slender and pretty as bugs' ears—took after their mother. Maria was slender and small framed compared to a lot of Indian women her age after having a bunch of kids. She reminded me some of my own mother. How that woman put together so much food amazed me, but she had lots of help and was used to feeding a bunch all the time. Sure beat the dried jerky and dried fruit I had in my saddlebags. Mother had made sure I had plenty to eat along with me before I left for Evarts, but it was mostly dried stuff she had prepared last summer.

The girls quickly cleared the table and Louie lit up a corncob pipe he pulled out of his vest pocket, and we were soon in a conversation about them black cows. I told him about seeing an ad in the *McIntosh Record* newspaper that I picked up at Bamble's Store in Thunder Hawk saying, "For Sale: Aberdeen-Angus, Entire Herd."

"They are new to this area, but from what I've heard and read about them in the *Dakota Farmer*, they should be the up-and-coming breed. I wanted to get in on the ground floor, so to speak, so I convinced Dad that we should buy them. He gave me the money for them but made it clear they were my venture and I'd have to pay back the money. I'll have to break horses and put up hay for him for the next ten years probably, so I sure hope they work out."

Louie said he knew my dad from back when he was a soldier at Fort Yates, sergeant in the Seventeenth Infantry, under Custer. (Nobody liked Custer because he hated Indians with a passion and he was a glory-hungry SOB.) "*Niyate kin toketu hwo*" (How is your father)?" Louie asked.

"*Slolwaye sni* (I don't know). I haven't seen him much, he mostly stays at Thunder Hawk, and Ben and I wintered over on the river and broke horses."

Louie felt like talking. He said he knew my mother and her folks, the Red Birds, and her uncles, Rain-in-the-Face, John Grass, and Gall. He told about Mother's dad getting shot along the Missouri River. Some of his band were shooting at a boat coming up the river and the boat people shot back, hitting him, and he fell into the water and no one ever found him again. Then her mother had married an army scout by the name of Sam McEldery. Mrs. Red Bird had four girls at that time, then she had a son John McEldery with Sam, and they lived at Fort Yates. He wasn't telling me anything new, but he was so engrossed in his story, I didn't interrupt.

"Well, I'll trade you my last Red Durham bull calf I get this spring for your first black bull calf and we can trade at the first snow this fall. OK?" offered Louie.

"OK," I said as we shook on it, "but if they all die the trade is off."

We both laughed and Louie said, "Right, I don't want no dead calf."

Brave Bear looked bored at our conversation and kept looking over at the girls, who were sitting around the heater stove and listening to our every word. The littler ones had already headed for bed. Finally, he said, "I'm going to go take care of our horses and roll our bedrolls out in the haystack, Louie, if you don't mind?"

"Go ahead," Louie said. "You are always welcome here but we are short on beds in the house. Take a lantern with you and give your ponies some oats too. There is oats in them barrels in the corner of the shed." Louie and I talked on for a while. He asked if I'd heard that the tribe was getting up a program to give all of us breeds that wanted to try ranching on the reservation some cattle to get us started or expand the herds we already had. "They're supposed to be bringing in four thousand head of Hereford heifers to the Agency at Fort Yates."

"Sounds good, Louie. I'll have to check it out," I said.

We could run four hundred head of cows and horses on the reservation for nothing, but any number over that we had to pay same rate as white leasers, and Dad was running what he could without paying any lease. Ben, Abe, and me was just trying to build up our herds. Our older sisters both married breeds—Sadie married Ben Defender and Annie married Charlie Gayton. I suppose they might be interested in the cattle deal too. Charlie just got elected the first sheriff of Corson County, but Annie could handle a few cows, and Sadie worked outside most of the time anyway. Dad had given her a few cows when she got married to Dick Track Hider, but she left him and then married Ben. We all thought she lost her sanity. Sadie loved kids, and her and Dick couldn't have any, and Ben already had some. Mother said that was why Sadie took up with Ben. Dick was really a swell guy and he always treated Sadie good, too. But anyway, her and Ben moved over by Kenal, so don't see much of them, probably a good thing.

I was getting sleepy too but couldn't be rude to Louie, and he sure seemed to want to talk. Louie told us that awhile back the Agency gave out a bunch of stuff. "Much of it was strange to us," he said. "One item in particular was a large white porcelain pot with a lid on it. Maria was cooking up soup in it one day when Henry Peck, a neighbor from over on Black Horse Creek, came along. We asked him in for dinner and he came in, looked at that pot, and lost his appetite. Wouldn't eat a thing," Louie said without expression. "Henry said that pot was a piss pot used at night so you don't have to go outside. You are supposed to keep it under your bed in the daytime, not cook in it!" Louie laughed and said, "I told him we use it for that too. But we really thought it was for cooking. Well, it's getting late. If you want to join Brave Bear, you are sure welcome, and breakfast is usually around six or daylight, whichever comes first."

"*Waste* (good night)," I said and headed out to the hay. Brave Bear had left the lantern lit hanging in the shed. Good thing too, 'cause it was pitch dark and starting to drizzle. I located my bed-roll, Brave Bear had it rolled out in a good spot about ten feet past his and he was already turned in. I wasn't sure if he was awake but I didn't say anything and tried to walk real light, but regardless he wouldn't sleep through anyone walking near him. Figured if I located my sleeping spot I could blow out the lantern and find it in the dark, and I did too. It felt good crawling into a warm dry place to sleep, a lot warmer than out under a tree with them cows, and it did start raining so would have been a miserable night out there. Good thing my friend caught up with me!

I was about half-asleep when I heard soft voices. Couldn't see a thing but the voices were coming from his direction and it sounded like a woman. Knowing my friend, I wasn't too surprised.

He always seemed to have a way with women. Even back at Indian school he was popular with the girls, and we had to fight back-to-back several times because he paid too much attention to some white boy's girlfriend and her beau would get jealous and pick a fight with Brave Bear. Mostly it was us breeds against all the white boys, and we were usually outnumbered, but we always managed to hold our own and get out of it with our hide still intact. Somehow, he had persuaded Lizzy and Alice to slip out and visit us. Someone stumbled and fell right on me, I suspected it was Lizzy, but couldn't tell in the dark, and before I could say anything there was a slender body shinnying under my blanket and snuggling very close to me.

She whispered in my ear, "Can't stay long; we are supposed to be in the outhouse. Left the lantern hanging there so it'll fool the folks for a while."

The morning broke clear and bright. It had stopped raining, and the sun was almost up when we rolled out of our bedrolls, gave our horses some oats, and headed for the house and a hot breakfast. We didn't have to knock. Louie met us at the door and said, "Come on in, the missus already has hotcakes and bacon and eggs on the table."

Maria said, "Good morning, boys, did you sleep OK out the in the haystack?"

"Sure did. I'm glad Brave Bear talked me into coming over here with him last night. Thanks," I said, and we sat down to a breakfast second to none, in my opinion. We finished off breakfast with a big hot cup of coffee, and when no one was looking I slipped a $20 bill under my plate. Brave Bear seen me though and he slipped a bill under his plate too. Then we headed for our horses, thanking them as we went out the door. None of the kids were up yet, not even the older girls. Louie came out in the yard as we were riding out and shook hands again and said, "You boys come back anytime."

The misses came to the door and said, "You boys are invited to a pie social at the Gopher School this Saturday night. Lizzy and Alice will be taking baskets. They would be thrilled if you boys would come and buy their baskets."

"Hey, thanks. We'll be there!" Brave Bear yelled, as we tipped our hats and hit a gallop out of the yard.

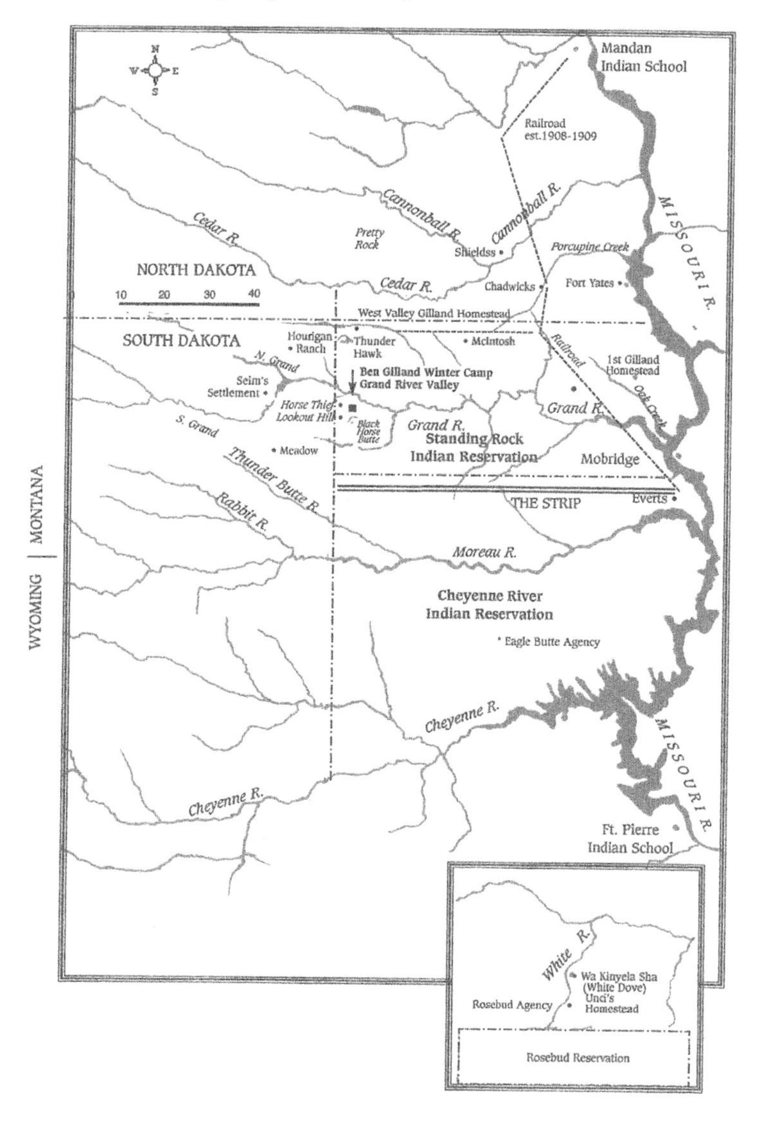

Map 1. The West River Country Showing "The Strip."

CHAPTER 5

Rabbit Creek Justice

"When we get your cows gathered again, Bob, I'm going to head on up the Strip and on over to Boyd Hall's place south of Rabbit Creek. Need to pick up a horse," Brave Bear said. It seems that he and Ben were over at Smokey Sebastian's place in Meadow about a month ago and some of them sodbusters were in there playing back east music on the nickelodeon. It was against the law to sell whiskey to Indians and we couldn't get a drop on the reservation, but we could buy whiskey at Smokey's.

"Ben got ticked off at them and I sorta helped him throw them out," he explained. "That music was still playing so Ben pulled out his six-shooter and put six holes in that song player thing. That got Smokey pretty upset and he pulled out his old shotgun and ran us both out of there and told us not to come back. About that time, we seen the town sheriff a coming so we swung atop our horses and headed east. Ben was too drunk to ride fast and that sheriff was gaining on us, so I told Ben to keep going as fast as he could, and I held back 'til that sheriff was getting pretty close, then I headed my horse south. That dumb-dumb came after me, but I was like a *siyo* (grouse) lame-ducking it along when you get close to its nest. The further he came, the better I got, and the faster my horse went. I lost him somewhere around Rabbit Creek, so I went on over to

Boyd's and left my horse and took a fresh one and went back to the reservation. Boyd knew that town sheriff and said he would send him packing if he came a snooping around his place, and I think he probably did.

"Anyway, I'll get my horse and head back, probably stay at Charlie Duncan's a day or two and be over to your place Friday night or Saturday morning. Have plenty of hot water so I can take a bath and get spruced up for that pie social," he said with a laugh.

"I'll have plenty of hot water," I said, "but be careful down around Rabbit Creek. Some of them SOBs shot at me last time I was down there." Then I told him about last year. Our horse herd always winters around Black Horse Butte, but last spring I couldn't find them. I did find a trail where horses had been chased, so I followed it and caught up with our horses in a corral down on Rabbit Creek straight south of Chance, at that old Matador winter camp. My horse was pretty played out so I caught Barnie, a well-broke, chubby, bay gelding of ours, and saddled up and was just swinging on when three guys came out of their shack and hollered and started shooting. That really spooked the horses, and me, and old Barnie hit the pole across the gate first knocking it down, and out we went with all the other horses right behind. I laid real low to the horse's neck 'til we got out of rifle range then I swung around behind the herd and took them on home. Their horses were in the bunch too, so they couldn't catch up, leastwise not 'til they had mounts again. Didn't take their horses back either, I slipped them in with the bunch and ran them all up to Thunder Hawk and told Dad to do whatever with them. I think they went up to Powder River country."

It turned out that was Barnie's last ride. When we got to the river, the ice was going out and the Grand was close to a quarter mile wide. When old Barnie hit the deep water, why, he just went plumb under and left me a swimming for shore. I think I might have drowned too, but got lucky. Another horse came swimming by and I just grabbed on to a handful of tail and he pulled me to the bank. When I got there, I let go of the tail. I was sure cold and wet everywhere. The horses didn't go far when we got across the river, and I walked up to another one, and took off my belt and hobbled him and went looking for Barnie. I found him washed up to a sandbar about a half mile down river, on my side of the river so I got my saddle and bridle off Barnie and saddled up the other horse. I gathered up the other horses and went on home to Thunder Hawk. It was a warm day but I was still kinda wet when I got home.

I thought I needed to warn Brave Bear. "Watch your backside down in that country—they may think you are me," I said. "To most of them whites, all breeds look the same. I'll know where to come a looking anyway, if you don't show Saturday morning."

"Oh, Bobbie! I'll show all right," said Brave Bear lightly. Then he added in a more serious way, "Three rustling saddle tramps won't do me in, but I might make it a point to have a visit with them. If they shoot at me, I'll shoot back! Thanks for letting me know about them."

"Well, I can see a few of them black cows," he said, "Bet the rest are in that draw just to the west of the ones we see." The cattle were easy to get gathered, hadn't scattered even a quarter of a mile from where I had left them.

"If you want to head on, I can get these cows on home today. Besides, Ben and Abe are supposed to come meet me and help trail them home. I seen a couple of riders coming this way over just east of Black Horse Butte. Bet it was them. If it was, they should be showing any time now," I told him.

We headed the herd north through the gate and Brave Bear turned and waved and hollered, "Waste!"

I waved and said, "Thanks for the help," as I was closing the gate and leaving the Strip. It would be tougher going now without a fence to haze the cattle along. I was heading the cows down into Black Horse Creek, just about a mile east of the Black Horse headquarters, when I seen Ben and Abe coming down the hill on the other side of the creek. I was glad to see my brothers coming to help. These old cows were hard to trail alone.

"Good morning Ben, Abe. How've things been at home?"

"Good," Ben said, as he looked over the cattle. "Looks like you got a fat bunch of cows. Some of them look like they'll be calving within a week or so. We would'a been here sooner but that bronc

Abe is a riding went to pitching with him and bucked right into a bog. Took some doing to get him out again, but he hasn't tried bucking since."

Then he told me that Dad, Mother, my little sister Bessie, and Jimmie, who's now fourteen, all came down yesterday in the buggy. Mother and Bessie went to cleaning up our shacks right away. Abe rode out and helped Ott Black trail a bunch of horses to my place for us to get broke.

"Dad said you and I can break teams. He left Abe with me to ride them that he wants for saddle horses, but we are supposed to help Abe some too. The others headed back to Thunder Hawk early this morning. Dad's Scotch blood was a boiling. That damned Smokey sent the law over to collect for damages someone did at his bar last week—$600 worth. Charlie Gayton came over and talked to Dad, and Dad sent the money back with him, but he was sure pissed off about it. That's why he sent those horses down to get broke and he wants them broke pronto. He said that should keep us out of trouble for a month or so and to stay the hell away from Meadow," Ben said waving his arm toward Meadow to make the point.

"Well," I said, "you get too drunk anyway, Ben, and you always drink that fighting whiskey. Every time you get to drinking at a dance you get in a fight, then everybody gets to fighting and it just ruins the dance and takes the fun out of it for everyone. I'm tired of fighting all the time and it don't make any points with the women either, so quit that damnable drinking. Abe thinks whatever you do he can do too. When he gets a little older he'll probably follow in your boots, and Jimmie wants to be like his big brother Ben too."

Dad always did hate to part with any money and he never spent any foolishly, or at least not 'til he had sons. But he always had plenty if he wanted to drink or gamble with cards. "Ben," I said, "what you need is a gal like that Maude Williamson from up in Pretty Rock country. Settle down and get some little ones to keep you home. I seen you and Maude last Christmas at that dance in Thunder Hawk—you two were belly rubbing all the time! Her family are poor homesteaders but what the heck. I bet she's a good worker and she really likes you. You ought to think about it."

Abe had had enough of our conversation. "Let's get these cows a moving. It's still twelve or fifteen miles to go, and I want to get home before dark! I got horses to tend to when we get back," he grumbled.

We got the cattle though the corral gate at my place just as the sun was about to set. Abe dropped off at Ben's on our way by to take care of his horses. "You want to come in for supper?" I asked Ben.

"No, better get home. Abe will be trying to fix something and he can't even boil water without burning it. Suppose we have to get at breaking those horses tomorrow.""OK," I said, "have to pitch some hay over the corral tonight for these cattle, but I'll haze them over to water and move the rest of the cattle in the morning, then I'll be over." I told him that Brave Bear and I were planning to go to a pie social at Gopher Saturday night. "You and Abe can come along too, if you don't have other plans."

Ben said he'd think about it but had figured on going up north. "See you in the morning," and he swung his horse around for home. He only had a mile to go.

The sun was high overhead and it was almost noon on Saturday, but no sign of Brave Bear. There was plenty of hot water on the stove and the reservoir was full too, and I had already taken me a bath. So come on, Brave Bear.

My coyote jumped up and ran out the door, a pretty good sign that someone was coming. I don't know where that coyote came from, and he really isn't mine, but one day last fall when I came home he was lying behind the stove. I'd left the door a little open because I'd built up too much fire and it was really hot inside. As soon as I stepped inside, this coyote came right up to me. Scared me at first but I could see he still had a collar on and a chewed-off rope tied to it. He just sniffed at me then went back behind the stove and laid back down. He looked like he hadn't eaten in a month of Sundays so I fed him a whole half gallon jar of canned meat and a bowl of milk, and took that collar off. He's been here ever since, doesn't make up to anyone else though, and leaves long before they can get inside. I leave the door open a little and he can paw it open and skedaddle faster than a cat can blink an eye.

Riders on the open range near Standing Rock Sioux Reservation between 1900-1910. A house with two chimneys shows in the background. Photo by Frank Bennett Fiske used with permission of the State Historical Society of North Dakota.

Brave Bear came a walking in with a big grin on his face and said, "Well, let's get with it. I've sure had a craving for pie the last couple of days!"

"Let's eat some stew," I said, "and then you can take a bath while I hitch up the team. We just as well take the buggy; you can pony your horse along behind if you don't want to come back here after the social. With the buggy, we might even get to take a couple of gals home. It's a nice day for a buggy ride, but it'll take us most of the afternoon to get over to Gopher. Anyway, how're the Halls and Duncans?"

"Not much happening at Hall's, but Boyd sure had my horse grained up good," he said. "I stopped by that shack on Rabbit Creek, the one where you picked up your horses. Boyd said everyone in that area had had some dealings with those three and all of them bad. He was sure they were into horse rustling and probably cattle too. So I told him I would look around and see if they had any horses with brands I recognized—and they did. When I rode into the yard, two of the guys were out by the corral, so I just rode up to them and asked if they had any stray horses, some of the folks over east were missing some. The guy I was closest to said, 'Hell no, we don't have any extra horses here.' So I asked if he'd mind if I took a look. The second guy spoke up then and said, 'Damned right we do, and get your stinkin' injun ass out of here while you still can. Aren't you the SOB that stole a bunch of horses from us last spring?'

"Before I had a chance to even say anything, there was a shot in the air. I looked around at the other one coming out of the house and he had a shotgun pointed right at my middle. He had shot over my head, but said, 'Get off that horse, you're a dead man as soon as you get away from that horse.' I felt a sick chill come over me as I realized how dumb I'd been, getting myself into a fix like this. I knew he wasn't bluffing and he was about to shoot for dead center just at any time. The hair on the back of my neck was standing up by now, I was sure scared. The other two started reaching for their six-shooters. It would have to be fast action and a whole lot of luck if I was going to get out of this one.

"I turned my horse broadside of the shotgun fellow and came off fast with my Colt in my hand. The first one had his gun right at me when I shot him dead center. He went sprawling back, dropping his gun, on his way to the ground. The second guy was still trying to get his pistol out of his holster, when I put one into his upper body. Didn't even watch him anymore, but spun under my horse's neck and fired a round at the guy with the shotgun. He fired as he was going back but shot high. When he hit the ground, he dropped his gun, then I looked back at the others to see if they were still aiming at me but they both were laying real still. I checked the shotgunner and he wasn't breathing so I checked the other two and they were in the same condition.

"Now, what the hell to do? I looked around and spotted an old root cellar that had been cut into a bank behind the shack. I knew I couldn't go to the law. Who would believe me? They'd probably hang me, or lock me up again, and I'd had too much of that already. So, I threw all three of them into that old root cellar, then I tied a rope around the top frame of the door that was holding up the other poles holding up the roof, and tied my rope hard and fast to one of their saddled horses that they had standing by the corral, and whacked him on the rump. He really took off and hit the end of the rope hard and that whole door came flying out and all the dirt that was on the roof came a tumbling down into that cellar hole. Covered those boys up slicker than a whistle.

"Then I took some tree branches and drug them across the yard several times to cover all the tracks and rounded up all the horses and took them over to Charlie Duncan's. There were several brands on the horses that I knew—LeRoy Flying Horse's, and Duchenaux's, and Bob Bobtail Blue Bear's, Lloyd Long Chase's, and even three of your dad's. I think they all came off the reservation. I told Charlie those with saddles on were just running loose with the other horses and he could keep them until their owners came around to claim them. Of course, I knew that to be pretty unlikely. The others, I just kicked east, back onto the reservation.

"You're the only one that will ever hear this story," Brave Bear said. "I know you'll keep a lid on it," and then without a pause, he switched to a gentler subject.

CHAPTER 6

The Gopher School Pie Social

It wasn't all that far over to Gopher, so we had us an easy buggy ride with some more time for talking along the way. "I was seeing a white gal some time back and she insisted that I teach her some Indian words," Brave Bear began. "So I did and one of the words I told her how to say was *canhanpi* (sugar). We were gathered around a bunch of friends at a celebration, and I introduced her, then she put her arm around me and said this is my '*sanhanpi* (red juice, from a woman)." I quick said, she meant *skuya* (sweetheart), and everyone laughed and I knew why. But I never told her the difference! I laughed and said, 'I'll shorten it a little and just call you *luta* (red) then!'"

It seemed like a good time to tell him that I had found out the other day what those circles of stones on some of the high hills around here mean and what they were used for. Mother had said they were a *womime wocekiya* (prayer circle) and were considered a sacred area and to leave them alone. But I overheard a group of homesteaders up at Thunder Hawk talking. One of the fellows was telling the others that a *real* Indian (Paul Red Fox) had told him this, so it had to be so. He said that Paul had told him, "Those rings of stone on the high hills were put around the bottom of the tepees so the wind couldn't blow them over and they wouldn't get any rain inside. Buffalo never attacked them up there either, and in the wintertime the snow always blew away from the tepee so they never got snowed in and couldn't get out!"

I said to Brave Bear, "Can you imagine anyone walking down a hill over a quarter of a mile and carrying water and firewood back up that hill every day? Where would they find a bush to get behind for an *oihe tipi* (outhouse)? I have seen some of those 'tepee rings' sixty feet in diameter, and some egg shaped and as much as forty feet wide and sixty feet long. It would be like watching a circus to see those boys try to fit a tepee under those stones. I just nodded and left them thinking that story was real."

"Well, when I wasn't at that Indian school," he said, "we lived in a tepee, and we always had it set up in a low area, close to water and timber. In the winter, we even tried to set up right in the timber so we'd be in shelter too. I doubt if you could get a 'real Indian' to even go near the top of a hill when there is lightning—all the Indians I know have a lot of respect for lightning. Some things are better left alone when it comes to explaining them to some of those white easterners that are coming into this county. They wouldn't believe a half-breed, anyway!"

When we pulled into Gopher, there was already a bunch of buggies and several saddle horses tied in different places around the schoolyard and a crowd of people standing around in front of the schoolhouse. Gopher was just getting settled, but it already had a post office, blacksmith shop, and a store, besides the new school, which was by far the biggest building there. There was just a few houses, but they were planning on a lot more and built the school big so all the ranchers' kids from miles around could walk to a school. It was good for dances and socials and they even used it for a church. The new school needed a lot more books and chalkboards, and such, and a social was one way to raise money. The womenfolk liked to show off how good their cooking was at a social. The highest bidder got to eat with the gal that cooked the food, and the pretty gals and best cooks raised the most money. Sometimes it was just pie or cake, but this one was for a full dinner basket.

"Hey, there's Alice and Lizzy," Brave Bear said just as the school mom came to the door and rang her school bell and beckoned everyone inside.

As we were heading in, I told Brave Bear, "*Nisnala ya yo* (you go alone)" on in and save me a seat by the girls, I have to hit the *oihe tipi*. The window at the back of the schoolhouse was open and I could hear women talking, so I kinda peeked in and seen a lot of baskets sitting on a long table, but I was surprised to see that school mom and another lady changing the ribbons on all the baskets. The baskets all pretty much looked alike but each girl had marked hers with a special ribbon. Alice said she would have a red ribbon on hers and them ladies took it off and put on a blue one, and Lizzy said her basket would have a pink ribbon, but it was changed too, now hers had a green ribbon. Boy! Glad I spotted the change—I'd better get inside and tell my buddy.

They already had a basket held up and were taking bids on it when I squeezed in between Lizzy and Brave Bear. I nodded and whispered "Hi" to Lizzy, then whispered to Brave Bear, "They changed the ribbons—Alice's is blue now!" He nodded and grinned like he always did. When they brought out the basket with the red ribbon, Alice's eyes just sparkled, but when Brave Bear didn't even bid, she gave him an angry look and slid over closer to her mother. After the bidding, she looked pretty puzzled when they placed it with its rightful owner. Then Lizzy's pink ribbon was sold and I didn't bid either, but I think she heard me tell Brave Bear so she didn't act too disappointed.

Most of the baskets brought from $3 to $7, but I had had to bid first on that green-ribbon basket and it was run up quite a bit to $22 before the other bidders gave up. Lizzy was the prettiest girl around and lots of the boys, including Arthur Vermillion and Joe Keeps Eagles, would have liked to share fried chicken with her. That basket had been the highest selling one so far. When they brought out the blue-ribbon one, I nudged Brave Bear, and he right away bid $20. Someone bid $21, and then Brave Bear bid $40, and no one else even bid. I said to him, "I think you could have got it for a $22 bid!"

"Yah," he said, "I think so too, but I don't have any one-dollar bills."

We did get the right baskets and the girls had really put together a great meal—fried chicken, biscuits, and potato salad, and a whole apple pie. Louie didn't get Maria's basket though and had to eat with the school mom; Maria ate with Henry Peck. We were the only ones getting the baskets that we wanted, but it was a good time and everyone else was joking about the mix-up. After everyone was done eating, some of the older ones started playing cards, but the girls wanted to take the little ones home and put them to bed and asked if we would take them. The older kids could come home later with Louie and Maria. Brave Bear said that it was OK with him but it was Bob's buggy. I didn't need any prodding. The girls told their mother what we were going to do and we were off with the girls and three of the younger kids. It wasn't far to Louie's place, maybe two miles, and it didn't take the girls long to get the little ones to bed and come out with some blankets for us to sleep on. I slept particularly sound that night dreaming of Lizzy wrapped in a blanket that she had had been pretty well warmed up for me.

What a way to be woke up! Someone was in the shed ringing an old cowbell. The sun was just coming up as Louie hollered at us, "You boys better roll out. The missus has breakfast on the table." Well, I needed to get home anyway, and Brave Bear said he wanted to go on over to Fort Yates. I think he just wanted to let the dust settle out west for a while.

As we scrambled to get to the table, Maria was serving up thick slices of bacon, plate-sized hot cakes with lots of butter and choke-cherry syrup, eggs fried in the bacon grease, and plenty of hot coffee. As we were finishing up, Brave Bear said in a mischievous way, "Maria, you're such a good cook; I think I'll steal you from Louie."

Maria replied, "Well, I'd go, but Alice did most of the cooking!" We all laughed at that one, but Brave Bear looked a little flushed and seemed to be at a loss for words.

Louie spoke up with, "Can you boys cut horses?" He knew we could, because, we had cut horses at the Indian horse roundup at Flying Horse's place last year. I had been cutting horses since I was about ten years old. Dad insisted that us boys cut our own horses and calves, and he always looked over our shoulder to make sure it was done right. I'd never lost anything to my knife yet.

So I said, "What's on your mind, Louie?"

"Well, I got a half a dozen stud colts in the corral that I would like to have cut. A couple of neighbors were coming over this morning to help throw them, but none of them ever cut a horse." I thought, he was as bad as my dad for manipulating! He knew we were coming over and would sure enough stay over so he figured he'd put a little work in our fun. A boy can't have too much fun, might ruin him or something; anyway that's seems to be the general consensus of some of these older gentlemen.

"Sure, we can do that for you, Louie," Brave Bear spoke up. We finished off our coffee and headed for the corral. Felix Fly, Roy Flying Horse, and Joe Bobtail Blue Bear came a riding in about the time I had finished making a wood clamp for the operation, and we went to work. There were a few more than a half a dozen, more like eighteen, and it took us all morning. Louie insisted that we come in and have a meal before we left, but it didn't take us long to eat and get out and harness and saddle up and head for the trail before he came up with some other little chore he needed done. Even though Louie had hoodwinked us into cutting horses for him, we had each slipped a bill under our plates to thank Maria and the girls for all the good food.

Louie came out in the yard as we were heading out. "I was supposed to tell you, the tribe has a horse roundup planned over at Chadwick's and want you boys to cut for them. They will pay a dollar a head, and there will be several hundred head to cut. Good thing you boys got in some practice—wouldn't want you to show up rusty!"

I thanked Louie for the news, then Brave Bear headed northeast and I headed northwest.

CHAPTER 7

Horse Cutting at Chadwick's

Back on the trail home, I had a lot of time to think, and that Lizzy kept popping up in my thoughts. It was sure getting blue in the west—I'd be lucky if I didn't get caught out in the rain. I hoped my cows got located; I'd hate to have them drift off and get caught out in the open in a storm. And I hoped none of them got stuck in a bog.

Over the years I had pulled several cows out of mud holes, most of them with my horse, but the first one was a little different. My pony couldn't get her out so I caught Dad's bull and saddled him and led him, and he just pulled that cow right out of the mud. He was a gentle bull. The winter before, my job was to take care of the bulls, and this particular one, I had led him for a while, then I started riding him down to water and back. That was back a few years, when I was about twelve. Just my luck, about the time I got the cow out of the mud, Dad came along and seen the whole operation. He sure gave me hell, said to never trust any bull!

"Bulls and men are a lot alike in some ways," Dad said. "You just can't think that because they're sometimes gentle and quiet, they're always going to be gentle and quiet. They can surprise you any time. They follow their own instincts and that may not be the same as the direction you are wanting to go in. And the quiet ones can be the worst," he said, his voice rising up for emphasis. Sometimes, when I was older, I thought about what Dad said that day.

I was hoping Ben got back from up north. Abe would take care of the horses but he wouldn't do anything with the cattle. Ben always watched the cattle like an old mother hen watched her chicks. The team was getting fidgety—either they sensed a storm a coming or just wanted to get home to a pan of oats. We were going home a lot faster than we left, anyway.

It was midafternoon when the buggy came to a stop by my shed. I still had time to gather up the cows and get them fed so they would stay around and go into the shed if it did start snowing. With the cattle fed, it was time to head for the house where old coyote was waiting at the door—suppose he wanted to get in to a warm place to sleep. I started to haul in a good supply of wood before it got all wet. The weather was sure enough going to do something; it'd already started to rain.

The storm came in from the southwest, started raining in sheets, and the wind came up strong. About midnight it started sleeting, and by daybreak it was snowing so hard you could only see about ten feet. What a storm, who would of ever thought! It should be spring. The temperature dropped steady all day; it started in the sixties with grass green all over, but the next day was a whole different world. By night it was ten degrees and getting colder; the snow and wind seemed to be getting worse. About daybreak, the wind switched to the northwest and then it really snowed and the temperature plummeted to minus thirty degrees, with a forty-mile-an-hour wind. Too cold for a man or beast to survive outside for very long. I couldn't even see my shed, let alone try to get out to it. Nothing to do but wait it out. The evening of the third day, it started letting up. I dreaded what I might find after this storm.

It was a clear sunny morning and the wind had stopped, but it was still biting cold. I hotfooted it out to the shed; there were seven of my original twenty-five cows standing there but not a black hide anywhere. I saddled up and rode over to Ben's to see if he had made it back. He and Abe were just heading out to assess the damage. Ben said, as I rode up, "Hell of a storm. You get your cows in the shed before it hit?"

I said that I got them up by the shed and fed them but there were only seven old cows in the shed this morning.

"Me and Abe will check on mine over west then swing around to Thunder Hawk Creek and Cyclone Creek, and the timber lot to check on Dad's. If we see any of yours, we'll stop and let you know on our way home," Ben said.

I headed east not knowing which way the cows went but for sure they went northeast or southeast. They would have gone with the wind, but did they leave when the wind was in the southwest or northwest? I seen three cows standing in the northeast corner of my homestead quarter that I had fenced. The snow had blown away from them but they weren't trying to go anywhere. Thought to myself that's kinda strange. I would a thought they'd be hungry enough to want to go eat. When I got up to them, they were frozen stiff and still standing!

I rode on the rest of the day and the next and the next but never found a black cow anywhere. All I could figure was that they must have drifted to the river and tried crossing and drowned or froze before they could get back out. Why hadn't I listened to Dad and not even bought them black cows, or why didn't I wait 'til after the cows calved and shipped them by rail to Thunder Hawk and trailed them south? Been closer that way, but saving on rail freight was the main reason to get them early before they calved. Baby calves are hard to trail—they would a been trampled if they were loaded on a boxcar with their mothers. Dad didn't want getting those cows to interfere with us haying, but at least the weather wouldn't have killed them.

The weather warmed and the snow melted as swiftly as it had come. Even that whelp of a coyote left the last day of the storm and was now gone with the wind! No sign of the snow was left when I rode up at Chadwick's for the roundup. The Agency had gathered up all the horses on the North Dakota side of the reservation—between two and three thousand horses were bunched there. Ranchers and hands paid by the Agency were sorting by brands; they fore-footed all the young horses that didn't have a brand and cut all studs. There were a lot of Indian cowboys on horses and a bunch more on foot. Tom Powers was there, and the Vermillion brothers, and Felix Fly. One cowboy would rope the horse by the forefeet, tie up one hind foot with a double half hitch, and the other cowboy would roll the horse over with the rope under it and wrap it around all four feet from the back side. It required fast teamwork and Felix was really good at roping, but Tom, as usual, mostly wanted to show off. All the boys knew their own horses and would run out with a branding iron when one of theirs hit the ground.

Branding two per minute at the Standing Rock Agency about 1908. Photo by Frank Bennett Fiske used with permission of the State Historical Society of North Dakota.

Brave Bear was already there and busy at cutting studs. I swung off and into action right away, and never got a rest 'til they broke for lunch, which was a little after midafternoon. There was washtubs of hot water and bad smelling disinfectant so we could keep our hands and knives and clamps clean. We used clamps that were hinged with bailing wire on one end and hooked with a loop of wire on the other end. Dad always said keeping everything clean was why he'd never lost a horse he'd cut.

"I heard you lost all your black cattle, Bob," Brave Bear said when we took a break. "If that isn't the damndest luck! Now what're you going to do?"

"Really haven't decided what to do," I said. "I heard the tribe was going to give out cattle next spring, but in the meantime, I was kinda thinking on going out to Montana to work on a ranch out there. Maybe I can make enough money to at least pay Dad some interest on the money I owe him. Ben and Abe can keep up with the work Dad has to do, and besides, Dad will be awful hard to be around this summer, after me losing his money on those dang cows. Ben just cost him some more money the other day too."

Then I told Brave Bear about how Dad had to bail out Ben and Blacky Stoner. "They were out at Miles City—just got back a few days ago. Blacky Stoner had worked for different ranches around and seemed to know something about horses. Dad had bought a string of horses out in Montana and sent Ben with Blacky out to trail the horses home. They took the train out with their saddles and bedrolls along with them on the train. Some of the horses in the bunch were broke to ride and they were supposed to saddle up and trail the rest back to Thunder Hawk. They got a room and were going to head back early the next morning, but you know Ben. Seems that Ben and Blacky headed for trouble rather than work. They left their saddles and gear in the room and decided to go have one drink before turning in. Well, it ended with a fight in the bar and the boys ended up in the jailhouse. They didn't have enough money to pay for the damages in the bar so Ben wired Dad by telegraph for some money. He was a mad Scotchman! He took the first train out there and got them out of jail and paid the damages. He took them right to the horses and made them saddle up. Then he opened the gate and the rest of the horses headed out of the corral like a bunch of mustangs.

"Get them horses to Thunder Hawk and don't even think about stopping at any town between here and there. If you get in trouble one more time, you'll rot in jail before I get you out again. If it weren't for those horses I'd a left you out here this time!" he told them in a voice that meant business. Dad didn't make idle threats. He always said, "If you tell someone something, you'd better be man enough to back it up, because sure as hell you'll have to, and usually when you least expect to." Ben knew he had pushed Dad to his limit and there wouldn't be any more bailouts. Ben said Dad was still mad as hell when they got the horses back to Thunder Hawk, so Blacky headed out for Selfridge and he headed back to his homestead. Ben figures to keep a low profile for quite a while.

"Maybe I'll go with you out to Montana; every time I turn around someone is trying to haul me off to jail in these parts," Brave Bear said. "Yesterday morning, when I was coming over here I was going up a draw over in them Porcupine Hills and a bullet hit the tree right beside me. Sure got my attention in a hurry! There were two want-a-be bounty hunters coming down the draw right at me and both started shooting but were piss-poor shots. Kept missing me anyway, but I had time to pull up my Colt and didn't miss. I just pulled the gear off their horses and turned them loose and left them boys lying in the bottom of that draw. That area isn't traveled in much. Doubt if anyone will find them for years.

"The Indian police at Fort Yates got after me too, right after that storm. I was spending some time with friends there and someone must have seen me and told the police. Anyway, sure glad I could run like hell. I seen them coming quite a ways before they got to the house and I hit the back door a running, and across the river I went zigzagging bullets all the way to the other side. They gave up the chase when I got to the other side. I had my horse in a thicket over there so I rode back out in the clear and waved at them boys, and went on over to Pollock," he said, demonstrating with a wave of his hat.

When we were at that Indian school, I'd been on the track team. I could run the hundred meters in about ten seconds and Harry Fast Horse could run it in nine. Brave Bear could outrun both of us, but he wouldn't go out for track. I told him if he would'a tried back at school, I bet he could'a ran a hundred meters in seven or eight seconds.

"Bob," Brave Bear said, "I could run it faster than that if bullets were chasing me!"

Turkey Track Bill came along about then and he said that he'd heard that Brave Bear outran the Indian police bullets crossing the

Missouri awhile back. We all laughed, and Brave Bear said that they didn't hit him anyway. Turkey Track Bill wasn't an Indian but was married to one and came over to help rope, and he was dang good at it too. He had came into this country with the cattle drives from Texas and worked at the Turkey Track cattle outfit, which had run sixty thousand cattle in the open range days. He was working for the Bicycle Ranch over in Pretty Rock country, but he had helped with the gathering horses and had some horses in the bunch too.

"Well, Bob," Brave Bear said, "Where're we going to sleep tonight?" Before I had a chance to answer, he said he had us invited to stay with the Goodreaus, over at Porcupine (about four miles away). They didn't have a haystack but had an extra tepee and the womenfolk would keep us fed up real good. I said that I hadn't made plans for sleeping yet but that sounded as good as anyplace else we could find in these parts.

There were a lot of women helping out with the food to get everyone fed that had showed up for the branding. Two of them, Babe and Florence Goodreau, were about our age and single and pretty all over more than anywhere else. We'd known a lot of other Goodreaus from Indian School, including Snooky and Bunky. Babe and Florence were both really smart in school; Snooky and Bunky were smart enough too, but were always in trouble for fighting. They were both dang tough and I was glad we were friends; I'd hate to have to see if I was tougher. Brave Bear and I rode to their place with the boys. Mr. and Mrs. Goodreau and the girls had driven back earlier in their buggy, and before they'd left said that supper would be ready about sundown. It was just about that time when we turned our horses in the corral and pitched them some hay and headed for the house.

The table was set out and they weren't short on food. Mr. Goodreau greeted us with, "Boys, you're just in time, grab a place at the table." As we were eating our fill of barbecued beef, baked beans, fresh baked bread, and pies made from berries that had been dried last summer, Mr. Goodreau told about their last guest, "It was kinda funny the other day when Acey Cottonwood came by and stopped for dinner. The missus had just gotten a jar of homemade horseradish from our neighbor to the south, Mrs. Mike Haider, and it was in a mayonnaise jar. I passed it to Acey, who took it and spread it on his bread really thick, and took a big bite. As tears rolled down his cheeks, Acey said in a deep voice we could hardly hear, 'You should 'a told me!'"

Then Mr. Goodreau started talking about Paul Red Fox who was the biggest storyteller on the whole reservation. Paul had stopped by to tell Mr. Goodreau that he'd just saved all his cow herd—seems the cattle were all lined up along one of them new fences that the homesteaders had put up and a thunderstorm came along and he had seen lightning strike that fence down a ways. He was between the strike and Mr. Goodreau's cows, so he jumped off his horse quick and cut the wires just before the lightning got to him, and it saved all them cows. Paul was pretty fast (according to Paul, anyway).

One time he told that old Pious Big Shield got him to go along and run out and grab prairie dogs. They were pretty short on meat so Pious wanted to get some dogs to eat. Pious was a good shot but every time he hit a dog it would fall down into the hole, so he got Paul to go along and try to run out and grab the dog as soon as he shot, so it wouldn't get away. Well, Paul said he got ready and just as he seen Pious squeeze the trigger, he took off and ran, grabbed the dog and lifted it up, then the bullet hit the dirt right where the dog had been! Now that is fast. Paul and Acey were at Indian school too, so we were well acquainted with Paul's stories. Paul really wasn't too fast a runner; several of us boys could run circles around him, but we could'a swapped stories about Paul all night and probably never ran out.

After a while, I said, "It'll be a busy day again tomorrow, think I'll call it a night." Brave Bear was quick to excuse himself too.

Mr. Goodreau said, "The girls have blankets spread for you boys in that far tepee—don't get in the wrong one, or you'll scare the girls and then they'll come a screaming." Then he laughed and said, "Good night, see you in the morning." (I thought, Brave Bear, you son of a gun!) He had done it again; the blankets were spread all right, but them "screaming girls" were keeping them warm for us too!

We finished up early the third afternoon so I decided to head for home as soon as we cut the last horse; it sure had been an interesting few days. Brave Bear said he just as well head out with me as it would be nice to have someone along to kinda watch his backside, but I soon learned he had another reason too. They paid us and we hit the trail.

CHAPTER 8

Brave Bear's Feast

Brave Bear and I were a few miles from McIntosh, when he said he had a little job to do. It might take an hour or so and he could use a little help. He told me that Jack Gayer was telling him a neighbor of his had bought an expensive bull and had boasted, "No one is a going to steal my bull. Not even Brave Bear can get him away from me. I put him in the barn every night and lock the door." Jack had asked Brave Bear to help him prove this homer wrong, so I asked what they had in mind. Brave Bear said that Jack would have a wagon and another guy, Ben Irons, to help, but if I would go along and just pull guard and watch the team, they would do the rest.

"OK," I said, "but how the devil are you guys going to get that bull out through a locked door?"

It was well past dark when we got to Jack's place but it was moonlight so we could see pretty well. Jack and Ben had the team hitched and ready to go. As soon as they seen us, Jack said, "Now we can let the fun begin!" Brave Bear and I followed along behind the wagon. When we got to the place, Jack stopped the wagon out from the barn a ways, and said to me, "If you see or hear anyone coming out of the house, give a coyote yelp and head south with the team. We'll run that way and catch up."

I tied my horse to the back of the wagon and grabbed the lines, Brave Bear tied his horse along with mine, and the three of them headed for the barn. I didn't hear a thing for it seemed like an hour, but might have been a half hour. Then here came Brave Bear and Jack each carrying a quarter of beef that they laid in the wagon; they were off again but soon back with the other half. They went back and brought the hide with the guts in the middle and dumped the guts in the wagon and took off with the hide again. In a minute, they were back and we were a getting out of there! Jack and Ben headed for Bullhead, said they knew plenty of people there that could use some meat and tripe. Tripe's the lining of a cow's stomach (like a chicken gizzard), and it makes a good stew. Brave Bear and I headed west at a fast pace.

After we were safely out of any hearing distance, Brave Bear laughed and said, "I'd like to see that guy's face come morning. He forgot to lock his windows." Then he told me they hung the hide over his gate and laid the bull's head on his doorstep. "I'll get credit for this caper too, I'm sure—at least I'm guilty of this one—but you know it seems I get blamed for every wrong doing on this reservation. Why, if I did half the things I get accused of, I'd have to get around faster than Santa Claus on Christmas Eve!" he said laughing.

We were riding along now at a slower pace and Brave Bear felt like talking. "It was kinda amusing to me the other day; I came by this old Indian's place early one morning when he was just coming out of the house. He'd picketed his horse right in front of the house," he started off. "I greeted him and he seemed like a friendly sort but we'd never met. I right away asked why he had his horse right in front of the house. It was an old horse, half workhorse or something; I'd rather walk than be seen riding something like that. Anyway, he said he had heard that that half-breed, Brave Bear, was in the area so every night he put his horse by the house so Brave Bear wouldn't steal him!

"I said, 'Well, I'm just passing through, looking for work, but I'd heard Brave Bear was in jail over in Deadwood (and I had been but had just gotten out), so I think you can forget about him stealing your horse!' With this news, the old man said, 'Don't know of any jobs around, but come on in for breakfast.' I ate breakfast, slipped a $20 under my plate, and left. I had this well-broke horse, kinda lazy, but that old man couldn't handle a speedy horse anyway, so one night I just left that horse in his corral, and left a note attached to the gate, 'Compliments of Brave Bear.'"

Daylight was just breaking when we got to my homestead and we hadn't had time to sleep any—at least at Goodreau's we got a little sleep. We must have been asleep almost an hour, or maybe it was ten minutes, when, here was Ben pounding on the door. He came in and said, "Don't you guys know a lot of people die in bed! So don't be laying in bed all day or you might wind up dead!" Ben said that Henry Duncan needed some help cutting a few colts and he'd told him we'd be there early this morning, so we had better be burning leather.

No time for breakfast, but Mrs. Duncan would have plenty prepared for lunch. It was only about five miles over to the Duncan place, and we were there even before Henry was finished with breakfast, so we had to come in and eat and drink a pot of coffee. They were sure friendly folks. The Duncan girls could ride horse as good as any man. Last year I had been up on Horse Theft Lookout, a high hill about halfway between my homestead and the Duncan ranch. I had a pair of binoculars and I seen one of them girls, riding sidesaddle, ride over to a newborn calf and get it up acrosst her lap and ride on home. It might have been one of Herb Lyman's cows. I didn't go check. It was quite a thing for a woman—even most men would have trouble carrying a calf on a horse two miles or so. Mrs. Duncan went to cleaning up the kitchen, but Lora and Kittie were wearing pants and came out with us to work the horses.

There was plenty of help: Tom, Bill, Charlie, old Henry, and a young guy by the name of George Minges. He had just came from back east and had been friends with the Duncans when they were there. He had been studying to be a doctor, but he got the fever and almost died. He had came out here to get his health back. Really a nice sort, and very well educated, but he had lost every hair on his body; he looked like a peeled onion on top. He said that after the terrible blizzard back in 1887, three steers with Teddy Roosevelt's Maltese cross brand had been found alive just north a mile or so, so he figured he would homestead there. If them steers could survive that storm there, it'd be a good place to put a house.

Henry only had a dozen colts to cut and brand and we were done by lunchtime. After lunch, Lora said, "We seen a bunch of Juneberries over southeast and wonder if anyone would want to go along and help pick them. We'll make you a pie if you do." Well, I liked Juneberry pie, so I was quick to volunteer, and Brave Bear said sure, he'd go too. Ben said no, that he'd better get back; he'd left Abe to riding some broncs and figured he'd best check on him. But I think he had someone else on his mind, like Maude, and he probably didn't want a wild story getting back to her. George said he didn't think he felt up to it either (he did look kind of sickly and probably needed to rest). The brothers said they'd work to do, so me and the girls and Brave Bear headed out in Charlie's buggy.

I helped Kittie pick a couple of lard buckets full of berries and we dumped them in a bushel basket in the back of the buggy. Brave Bear and Lora were nowhere around—they had been picking up the draw from us so maybe they were just out of sight. Kittie said, "It's getting hot, I'm going to take a blanket and go sit down the draw under the trees. You can keep picking or join me." If that was a choice, it didn't take me long to decide. We were soon resting on her blanket under the trees, then she said, "I'm still hot. Aren't you hot with all them clothes on, at least take off your shirt," So I did and she was out of her shirt and trousers both by the time I got my shirt off. The thought occurred to me if her dad comes along about now there'll probably be a shotgun wedding.

We managed to get back to the Duncan headquarters before dark and in time for supper, and then decided we had better get on for home. Boy, I thought a good night's sleep will sure fit with me. As we were riding along, Brave Bear said, in a real sober tone, "That Lora is sure a hot-blooded woman; she stripped off naked under the trees and laid on a blanket to cool off and left me to pick all those berries, all by myself."

I said with a grin, "Maybe you kept picking berries, but I doubt it! I looked over your way once and couldn't see either of you."

Brave Bear just laughed, "Now we'll have to go back in a day or two if we want a piece, of pie!"

I said that'd be OK—we'd stop back on our way to Montana.

Brave Bear came back with, "Sounds good, in three days we'll meet up back at Duncan's and head out from there."

As we came riding up to the corrals, we could see a light on in my log house. Now what? "Why don't you go check it out," Brave Bear said, in a whisper, "I'll just stay here with the horses in case it's a problem."

"Charlie Gayton!" I said loudly. "Hi, Charlie. How's sis? And the little ones? Is this a social call or are you on sheriff business?"

He grinned at that and said the family was fine, but the founding fathers at McIntosh wanted him to come and have a talk with me and Brave Bear about a butchering over east of McIntosh last night.

"I'm not much into butchering. Haven't butchered anything since last fall when I helped Ben butcher a beef for mother to can up for us, but it was one of Dad's steers and we did it in broad daylight," I said keeping my voice as loud as I could while stepping through the doorway. I mentioned that we were over at Chadwick's cutting horses for three days, finished up yesterday, and today we'd been over helping Henry Duncan. "I think we hardly had time to do any butchering."

Charlie said that he had promised the townsfolk at McIntosh that he would come out and take us back for questioning anyway. Brave Bear wasn't wanted for anything in Corson County, but he was wanted in Sioux County, North Dakota, for a suspected shooting, and horse stealing, and a few other suspicious happenings. "But, I won't hold him for any of them things," he said. "I just wanted you and him to answer a few questions. Where is Brave Bear anyway?"

"We rode home from Duncan's together and he was at the corral when I came in, so he'll probably be in as soon as he gets the horses cared for." Brave Bear didn't mention staying or going but I guessed he figured on staying the night. I asked, "Charlie, is that fresh coffee on the stove or is it still from last night?"

"I just made it. What was in the pot looked like mud." I poured myself a cup and refilled Charlie's cup. We finished off our coffee and still no Brave Bear. Charlie said, "I'd better go out to the corrals and find that Brave Bear; it's a long ride back to McIntosh yet tonight." I went along out with Charlie but when I didn't see Brave Bear's horse, I knew he had rode out into the night. I also knew Brave Bear would have no part in riding to McIntosh with the county sheriff, and there would most likely be a shootout between my best friend and my brother-in-law. I would be somewhere in the middle. I, for one, was sure glad he was gone.

Just as causal as I could I said, "He must'a decided to go on. You know, he never likes to stay at one place long enough to wear out his welcome." But in my mind, Brave Bear would always be welcome at my place and I was sure he knew it too. "Charlie, I sure hate the thought of riding clear to McIntosh tonight, but if you insist I'll saddle up a fresh horse."

We got to McIntosh after midnight. Charlie said, "I'm not taking you to the jail; you'll stay at the house with me and Annie."

Annie was still up when we came a walking in and she looked like she had fire in her eyes. She had Dad's red hair and his short-fuse temper, and I could tell Charlie was in for a tongue-lashing. "Hi, Bob," she said giving me a big hug. "There's an extra bed in the room with the boys. You go on in and go to bed; I want to have some words with my husband!"

I didn't argue with her. I was dead tired anyway, so went in and crawled into bed, my head didn't even hit the pillow when I heard her tie into Charlie. I couldn't hear all of what was said, but it seemed it was about dragging her brother all the way to town from his homestead and accusing him of something so ridiculous just to make himself look good with the idiots in town. I fell to sleep with Annie still giving Charlie hell.

Annie's little boys woke me in the morning with the excitement of seeing their favorite Uncle Bob sleeping in their room, and were all over me before I could get dressed. The boys and I went out to the kitchen together. Annie already had us a big breakfast fixed, but Charlie wasn't at the table.

"Charlie changed his mind," she said. "He doesn't want to take you to jail for questioning. He left earlier but said to tell you that you're free to go anytime you want."

When I got back, I told Ben about my plan to go to Montana and work out there for a while. I had to try to make some money and pay Dad back at least some, anyway. We'd tried riding at rodeos but that was a pretty iffy way to make much money. Ben and I were usually in the money but we had tough competition, like the Babe and Jack Mansbridge, Ike Blasingame, and a few others. And when we won, we'd have to party with the boys, and usually spent more than we made. No, better leave that rodeoing to Abe. Ben said that he would keep an eye on my homestead 'til spring, but I'd better be back in time to get in on some of them cattle the tribe was supposed to be giving out in the spring. I said I'd be back, probably before that.

"Maybe Dad will be easier to get along with by then," Ben said. "He sure has been a bear cat to be around lately. I'd go too if I didn't have to take care of my cows. I wonder if Dad wasn't having problems with his health. Mother said the other day that he'd been crabby with her too."

I thought to myself, probably more like money problems. Dad was very Scotch with money and Ben had cost him plenty lately.

"When I was up there the other day," Ben said, "they were mad at each other and wouldn't talk. Both of them were walking around the house like they was looking for something. When I asked what they'd lost, Mother said she was looking for her glasses so she could do some sewing, and the glasses were hanging up on her head. Dad said he was looking for his pipe, and it was hanging out his vest pocket.

"Anyway, Bob, stay out of trouble and I'll see you in the spring."

CHAPTER 9

Riding for the Montana Stockmen's Association

Being completely on my own was gonna be a new experience for me, but having a friend like Brave Bear with me would be some consolation. As I rode up to the gate on the west side of the reservation (about a mile from the Duncan's headquarters), he was already there waiting for me with the gate open.

"Hey, daylight's a burning. I been here for an hour or so. Kittie and Lora went north in a buggy with that bald guy, so let's just pass by the Duncans and head for Montana. Or do you want to stop and get a pie to take along?"

"Nah," I said, "let George have it. Montana, here we come! Have you ever been to Montana?"

"I passed through a couple of times but never stuck around long enough to do any work there," he said. What about you?"

"About the same with me. I hopped a freight train with my mother's brother, Uncle John McEldery, two summers ago and we went clear to California, but we didn't do much work either. It was an interesting trip—Uncle John knew a lot of people and places along the way. We stayed at the hobo jungle most places and it didn't cost much. After a week or so in California, we just hopped on a train and came home again. I had kinda forgot to tell my folks I was going with Uncle John and when we got home, we both sure caught hell from Mother and Dad. Mother burnt our clothes, and we had to take a bath and wash our heads and scrub down with kerosene. Mother was sure that we'd brought back lice and bed bugs and whatever else there was to catch in a hobo jungle. When I went to bed, Mother was still giving Uncle John heck, and he just left again and ran over to the tracks to catch another train."

There was several ranches along the way to Miles City that wanted help for a day or two but nothing for a month or more, so we were riding into Miles City without a job, but the day jobs gave us a little spending money. I didn't bring a lot of money with me, just what I'd gotten from cutting those horses at Chadwick's. Brave Bear probably had plenty though; he always seemed to have quite a bit of cash with him and wasn't shy at spending it either. We decided to head over to the first bar on the main street of Miles City to see if we could pick up a job. We weren't there long when a couple of well-dressed fellows came a strolling over to our table and offered to buy us a drink. I said, "Sure, have a seat, but they won't sell us a drink, just sarsaparilla. Said they couldn't sell Indians any liquor."

One of the fellows said, "Let's see about that," and waved the bartender over and ordered four shots of whiskey. The bartender brought the drinks and didn't say a thing about it.

We introduced ourselves and then I said, "You must be pretty important around here; that same bartender told us we couldn't drink in here."

The fellow that had ordered the drinks said, "I'm known pretty well around here. My partner, here, and I have one of the biggest ranching operations in these parts—that's why we came over to talk with you. We have a National Stockmen's Association out here and we'd like for you boys to come work for us. There's been a lot of rustling going on and we just can't seem to find out where our stock is going. So if you're interested, we'll pay you each $2 a day from the Stockmen's Association and whatever wages you get from working on the ranch you can keep. But we want you to work on different ranches. The average ranch hand gets about $30 and keep, but you boys look like you'd be worth twice that!"

Brave Bear let out his smile slowly, "What makes you think we can even ride a horse?"

Now the fellow that hadn't said anything spoke up with, "If you two aren't top-notch hands I'll kiss someone's bare ass! And I don't expect to do any kissing. We've worked with a lot of men over the years, and I think I'm a damned good judge of character. Right, Noote?"

"Right you are, Pete." Then Noote turned and said, "I bet you boys could hit a flea off a dog's ear a hundred feet away!"

Brave Bear grinned, "Bob has been known to hit a gopher off a running horse some tell me, but I never seen it. As for me, I can hit dead center of what I'm shooting at but can't hit a gopher from a running horse. Trouble is, I can never get that danged gopher to sit on a running horse long enough to get a shot at it!" We all laughed.

"You guys will do fine," Noote said. "If you want the job, just follow us out to the ranch. I'm going north and Pete is heading over to the south ranch. Meet us at the general store in about ten minutes; they're loading our buggies with supplies there and should be finished by then." They got up and out the door they went.

"Well, didn't take long to find a job. Which way do you want to go, north or south?" asked Brave Bear.

"Doesn't matter to me," I said, "long as the pay is the same. Suppose I can go north as long as I'm sitting on the north side of this table."

"Good idea. I always wanted to go south anyway—that south ranch might be in Wyoming or Texas. Let's meet up back here in a month—Saturday night, seven o'clock, OK?"

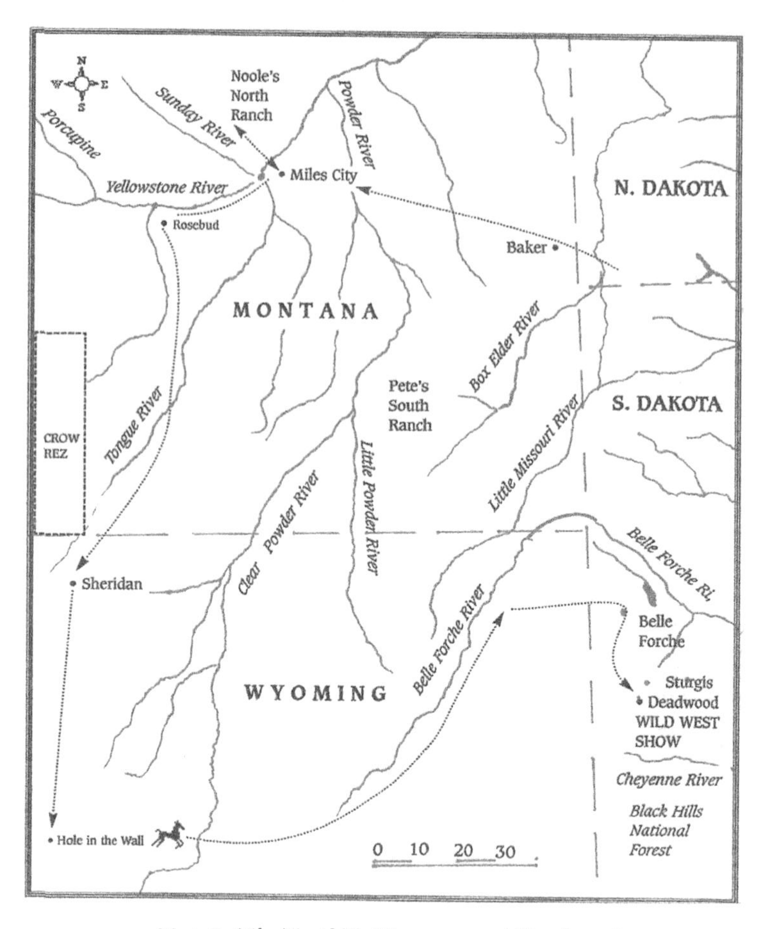

Map 2. The Trail To Montana and Deadwood

I agreed and we strode on out to our horses and headed for the general store. I followed that buggy on a winding trail northwest close to twenty miles. Finally, the buggy stopped in front of a big ranch house and three Chinamen ran out and started unloading the buggy. The boss got off the buggy and said, "Come along with me, Bob, and I'll introduce you to the boys and the bunkhouse." Then in a low voice, "Keep it under your hat about working *undercover.*" I met a crew of ten men, some looked like old hands, but a few looked like they didn't know the meaning of "cowboy up." The bunkhouse was plenty big and well kept, not a thing out of place, a lot more tidy than my log house back home. Noote said, "Don't let the looks fool you, the men aren't this tidy. We have some of those Chinamen come in each day and make up the beds and clean house. They cook a mean meal too, which should be about ready now, so let's get on over to the kitchen."

The kitchen was as big as most people's living rooms with a long table that could set at least twenty people at one setting. Noote took his place at the head of the table and motioned at a chair next to him for me to sit in, and in a jiffy, we had Chinamen bringing food at a steady pace. They were good cooks, but I couldn't understand a word they were saying. They did a good job of getting their point across though by just using their hands, and that I understood. (We weren't allowed to talk that way back at Indian school.) Noote said that he'd see us boys in the morning, and got up and headed for his easy chair in the living room, and me and the rest of the boys headed for the bunkhouse.

We were about halfway there when one of the guys turned around and said to me, "I ain't never slept with no damned stinkin' injun yet, and I'm not about to start now!" I knew those were fighting words and I would have to adjust his attitude a little, and the quicker I did it the less chance some of the others would express their feelings too. So I just stepped forward quick and gave him a short but hard fast left punch right between his right eye and his mouth. He went backwards and down like a chopped-off tree, and just laid there. The rest of the guys gathered around and a couple started trying to revive their buddy.

One of the guys standing closest to me said, "Bob, the rest of us don't share his feelings. No sir, you're on the payroll same as us and we'll make every effort to work with you. Come on with us to the bunkhouse. Maybe we can even teach you how to play some cards."

As we were heading for the bunkhouse, I said, "I don't know cards much. Tried poker a time or two but always lost my money so quit playing."

We hadn't gone ten yards when we heard someone coming at us from behind. I turned, expecting it was those other two or the one that I'd knocked out to the ground, but it was Noote. He had an expression on his face I'd never seen before, not really a mad look, more like determined. He stopped in front of them on the ground (the one knocked out was starting to regain consciousness now and was sitting up). He already had a handful of bills in his hand and counted off their wages and threw it on the ground by each one of them and said, "You boys are fired. I want you off this ranch just as fast as you can get off tonight. If I ever see you anywhere, I'll have Bob pierce your ears with bullets!"

I doubted if Noote would need me or my gun if he encountered them boys again. He was big enough and moved like a cat on a hot stove, so I'd place my money on Noote, if he ever squared off at anyone. The way he wore his gun belt low and at a natural swing with his arm told me he probably was plenty handy with his six-shooter. Noote followed along behind everyone to the bunkhouse and came in and watched the fired hands gather their personal belongings, which weren't much, and after they went out the door, he said, "If there's any of you that don't want to sleep with an Indian in this bunkhouse, just step forward and draw your pay." No one stepped forward, and after a minute, Noote said, "OK, then get some sleep and we'll be slapping leather early in the morning!"

After our "Chinese" breakfast, Noote said, "A couple of you boys go out and wrangle in that bunch of stud colts we've been going to cut all spring, and we'll see if our Indian friend here can cut a horse!" I didn't say anything but, I thought, 'If this is a test of my ability as a ranch hand then they couldn't have picked a better job.' I cut them horses in record time and I think it was a good impression on the boss. When we were done, he said, "You're the fastest I've ever seen with that knife. Good job, Bob."

A few days later, just as we were finishing up on breakfast, we heard the cooks yelling in Chinese. When we looked over there and seen what had happened, one of them had been washing dishes in the dishpan and had thrown a butcher knife in the pan too. He had ran his arm across the knife and cut it to the bone—blood was a gushing everywhere. He bled to death in just a minute or so and there wasn't a thing any of us could do about it.

A long month had gone by, and I was wondering how Brave Bear got along down south. I had just sit down at the table in that bar in Miles City when in walks the man himself. Before we had time to say much, in came Noote and Pete. Pete waved the barkeep over. He came with four shots of whiskey and left the bottle. Noote said, "You boys are worth your wages as cowhands, but you haven't caught many rustlers yet!"

"I've been watching," I said, "just haven't run into anything suspicious yet."

Brave Bear said that he had. Said he was way on the south edge of the ranch where there was an old line shack. Someone had been camping in it and it wasn't any of the ranch hands. "It was either five guys or one guy who ate five times because there were five dirty plates and cups at the table. No one was around, but I'm sure they were close by." He said that when he was in the house he felt like you do when you see a tick on you then lose him and don't know where he went, like you feel crawly all over more than anywhere else. Anyway, he said he was sure someone was watching him so he left, went back to the ranch, and figured he would slip down there some moonlight night. "But when I do," Brave Bear said, "I'd like to have Bob go with me to kinda watch my backside."

"Sure," Noote said, "just tell Pete and he'll come up and get Bob."

Pete said, "Maybe it was that big-footed apeman Brave Bear felt was nearby."

There had been a big write-up in all the newspapers about a hairy creature that some cowboys, out around Butte, had roped and got tied up. They hauled it into town and locked it in a jail cell. The story in the paper said the cowboys came up on this creature feeding on a deer and they snuck up and roped it. It was a female, and after a day in the jail its breasts started dripping milk, so they figured it must have a young one and they thought, if they turned it loose and followed it with fast horses they could catch maybe a whole family of apemen. So they turned it loose, and it outran those horses so fast that they didn't even see which way it went. They did have a picture in the paper of the creature. It looked about six feet tall with great big feet, long arms and legs, and hair all over, and they said it's hair was a sort of orange brown in color.

Brave Bear said, "An apeman would have kept a better house than that!" We all laughed. The meeting with the bosses was short—one drink, then they left.

I said to Brave Bear, "Well?"

He knew what I meant, so he said, "When I first got down to the ranch, two of the hands said I couldn't sleep in the bunkhouse. They said I could sleep in the barn; I was about to hang one on them when Pete stepped in between us and fired them on the spot. The rest have been an easy bunch of guys to get along with. There is even a reservation just over to the west where the ranch runs some cattle, and there are some mighty pretty Indian gals over there." I thought, now why doesn't that surprise me? Brave Bear had already found some girls even out here, but that was just the story with him ever since I had known him. Brave Bear said that he'd gone over there one night just to get acquainted, then went back just to visit a couple of times. "One family over there invited us to a family dinner any Sunday, if you would want to go. We can even go tonight!"

I just said that sounds swell, but I was thinking that he very likely has more than dinner on his mind. And I'll bet there just happens to be a couple of single daughters that need some help doing something!

Brave Bear said, "You know, I seen the funniest looking cattle the other day. Pete was having trouble with wolves killing calves, so he had some of these shaggy-haired long-horned cattle shipped over here, clear from his homeland of Scotland. He calls them Scotch Highlanders, and Pete claims he hasn't had any problem with wolves getting their calves!"

Fall was on us and still nothing on the rustlers. I had went with Brave Bear to that shack and all we seen was five guys sleeping, but they were the three that got fired up north and the two from the south ranch. Now, Pete had came up again and said that Brave Bear needed me to help him but didn't say what for. But I pretty much knew. It was dark when I rode in at the south ranch and Brave Bear was on his horse and met me at the corral with a fresh horse. As I was saddling up he said, "Let's head south. I'll fill you in as we go."

Brave Bear had followed tracks of cattle being chased to the area of that shack. That morning he quit trailing and sent Pete up for me. He said that with any luck, we could still catch up with them before morning, but he wasn't any too sure how old the tracks were; they might even be a few days old. There was a thin dusting of snow on the ground and a full moon so it would be easy going and even an "injun" should be able to follow them cattle tracks tonight. We finally caught sight of the cattle and five riders pushing them along. (We must have already rode over a hundred miles!) I guessed there was at least a hundred head of cattle, looked like mostly young cattle. I thought at least they were smart enough to steal prime stock. It was already close to midday and getting warm for the middle of February. They pushed the cattle down to a creek and to a ripple where the water was running and then they had a powwow. Two of them headed south, the other three stayed back, and were keeping the cattle bunched.

"Why don't you double back, keep out of sight, and ride on south too," Brave Bear said. "It can't be more than five or ten miles to Sheridan, Wyoming. Get to the telegraph office and wire Noote and Pete we caught up with their cattle thieves. Then, maybe get the sheriff to get some deputies around their stockyards and they should be able to catch these boys red-handed."

"Good plan," I said, and I back-trailed, keeping out of sight, and headed into new territory, and Sheridan. I zigzagged along, making sure I kept out of sight of the boys behind me and the two in front of me. I came into town on the east side and headed down Main Street until I spotted the telegraph office—it was just across the street from the sheriff's office. I got a telegram off to Noote and Pete, then went straight over to the sheriff, but he wouldn't believe me or maybe he had been bought off. At any rate, I wasn't going to get any cooperation from him. So I wired Noote and Pete again and told them Brave Bear and I would try to bring them boys in but they should at least send someone to help take the cattle back. Then I hightailed it back to Brave Bear.

He wasn't where he had been but was standing by his horse down where the three had been with the cattle. The cattle were drifting back north, and when I rode up to Brave Bear, I could see the three cattle thieves, one lying pretty close to Brave Bear and the other two a ways off, both lying still and dead-like. Brave Bear seen me coming and had turned around to face me.

"I thought you were just going to watch. What happened?" I asked my voice cracking with surprise and disbelief.

"You know," Brave Bear answered, "it gets pretty damned boring just watching three guys do nothing. I got tired of that so decided to come down and visit. At first, they were friendly enough, then this first one got off to my side and went for his gun, but I read his mind and was ready for him and I happened to get off a shot and he didn't. I stepped quick behind my horse and came around his back side and the other two over there were both aiming at me, so I fired a shot at each of them and they quit aiming at me."

"I thought I heard shots a couple of miles back," I said. "Well, I wired Noote and Pete, but that sheriff wouldn't help at all. He said that I was just making up a wild story and I'd better be out of his town in five minutes or he would lock me in his jail and throw away the key!" We were still pondering about what to do when our horses perked their ears up and looked south; we looked to see what they were a looking at and seen two riders heading west like a couple of scared jack rabbits.

Brave Bear said, "Damn, they must have seen their partners and didn't want any of the same."

"The three lying here are the ones that were up on the north ranch so the ones getting away must be your buddies from the south ranch," I said.

"They just think they are getting away. Let's be a riding," Brave Bear spoke, like he meant it. We rode hard but we just couldn't seem to gain much on those two, and our horses were sure getting tired.

"There's a ranch just over a little from us," I suggested. "Let's see if we can buy a couple of fresh horses and a bite to eat and pick up their trail again. It'll be moonlight and with the thin snow cover on the ground we should be able to catch them before midnight." The man at the ranch was as helpful as he could be, after we mentioned Noote and Pete had sent us after these fellows. He most likely knew them or at least their names and wouldn't take anything for the horses; just said we could swap back on our way back. (I think he just wanted us to stop back so he could find out the end results.)

Brave Bear said, "Them homers must have traded horses on the trail somehow. They've picked up steam on us and we have fresh horses." About then, we found out how they had traded horses; coming in our direction we seen two cowboys riding two wore-out horses at a snail's pace. When we got up to them, they said that two riders came at them with their guns drew and made them get off their horses, and they switched horses and were soon racing out of sight.

"We are the reason they were in such a hurry," I said, and I told them how we were hired by the Montana Stockmen's Association and had caught up with them stealing cattle, but they got the run on us and we needed to be going if we are ever going to catch them.

Brave Bear said to me, "Bob, I bet they are headed for the Hole-in-the-Wall, and if I'm right, they will have to head a little south soon so if one of us heads southwest and the other stays on the trail one of us should run into them."

I agreed with his plan.

"I'll head southwest," Brave Bear said. "You just slow her up a little and follow the trail and keep your eyeballs peeled in case they double back. Shoot if it looks like trouble and if you hear shots kick it in the ass."

I said, OK, but I really didn't intend to slow up any. It was well into the afternoon and I had been trailing along alone for three or four hours. Then I heard shots, not ahead but off to the south. I thought they must have turned south and sure enough, I hadn't went another quarter of a mile when I seen their tracks heading due south. I rode as fast as I could in that rough country but didn't hear any more shots, only those two. I rode another mile or so when I seen Brave Bear, just standing by his horse.

When I rode up, he mounted his horse and said, "We can quit chasing them."

"Looks like they tried drawing on you!"

He said, "I just stepped out in front of them and said, 'You boys are going back with me to jail.' They looked real surprised, but didn't seem to think much of my idea and started grabbing for their six-shooters. I just fired a round at each of them first and they dropped their guns and fell off their horses. I already unsaddled their horses and turned them loose. Let's get the hell out of here."

I said, sure but, which way, and he said that we were almost at the Wall, so we might as well go on in there and hole up for a few days and get rested up.

We rode in without any incident, but it sure was a dirty-looking mess. The place had a kind of forlorn and worn-down air. There were corrals with some skinny cattle and tired-looking horses and several cabins that had seen better days scattered around. It was like they were waiting for somebody to return but they knew that wasn't gonna happen. I thought to myself, 'What the devil has Brave Bear got me into this time?' But I figured he must have been here before. Sure enough, several of the guys there knew Brave Bear and came over and shook his hand.

"Who's your sidekick and what are you a running from this time?" said one they called Elzy. There was another called Kid and one named Laughing Sam, but no one said a last name and I sure wasn't going to ask.

Brave Bear said, "This is my friend, Red Eagle, and we just shot five guys that didn't agree with us so want to rest up a little without the law running us in to ask questions."

"Well, you came to the right place; there is an empty shack yonder," Elzy said as he pointed it out. "The boys that were there won't be coming back. They got shot up at a bank shoot-out over east. So stay as long as you like. Just don't take the big cabin up behind that pine tree 'cause that is Butch's cabin and he'll be back any day now. Butch don't like nobody else stayin' in his place. Oh, and Mustache Maude and Shady Sadie are the camp cooks in that first shack. If you want to eat with us, it'll cost you each a buck a meal."

Brave Bear said that would be fine and see you at supper. We headed over to our new home, which looked better inside than it did on the outside. Whoever those boys were, they had left it cleaned up, even had a couple of cots with clean sheets on them. Supper wasn't much but there was plenty of it, and after the long dry spell we had just been through any food looked dang good.

One of the shacks was used for a drinking and card playing place—drinks were a buck a shot, and the girls $5 a throw or $15 for all night, but homely took on a new meaning with them gals! They were as ugly as homemade sin, or even worse. We had one drink and decided we were too tired for any more of their excitement. When we got back to the shack, Brave Bear said, "Have you ever seen more ugly women?"

I said, "I can't recall ever seeing any quite that bad, and I bet they carry every kind of disease there is!" Brave Bear said that they couldn't pay him enough money to get him to sleep with them. I said that was my exact thought too!

We laid around there a couple of days, and the night of the second day Brave Bear had enough resting and said, "Let's get out of here first light in the morning."

"I'm sure for that," I said.

"Lets head up through the Crow Reservation on our way home, or do you want to go back to work for Noote?"

"I'm ready to head home," I said, "but which way is closest?"

"Probably back the way we came, but let's veer east a while so we don't have to ride by those boys we left laying on the trail. Maude said she would tell the locals about them when she went out for supplies, but no use taking a chance; with our luck we would probably run into the law and have to explain ourselves. Better avoid that area," he added.

I agreed. We managed to get back to the ranch where our horses were and spent the night there. Next morning, we ate, left a $20 bill under our plates, and were fast gone.

After we had rode a few miles east, Brave Bear said, "You know, it's about as close to Deadwood as to the Crow Reservation. Let's take a ride over there and see if they're still doing that Wild West show!"

"*Niyelo* (It's up to you), but only for a month or so." I didn't like the idea of hanging around too long.

"We won't stay too long. Besides, we could use a little excitement after working seven months on a ranch." Then he added with a grin, "I used to know a really pretty gal over in them hills."

CHAPTER 10

The Trail Home Goes through Deadwood

It was snowing hard when we rode up to the livery stable in Belle Fourche. We had the stableboy feed our horses and rub them down, and we headed uptown for some excitement. Brave Bear said that he knew a place to eat, "Let's have a bite, then we can do in the town!" I thought he meant a café, but he didn't. We went a walking down a back street and up to a house where he knocked on the door. A very pretty red-haired gal came to the door, threw her arms around him, and kissed him right on the mouth! I thought, well, guess he's been here before.

Brave Bear pulled back and said, "Marianne, meet a good friend of mine." She looked at me, and I shook her hand.

"Well, come on in," she said. "Any friend of Brave Bear's is welcome in this house!" Brave Bear told her we were going to get a bite to eat, then see what's happening up town. Marianne said, "You're in luck. I have plenty of supper on the stove." About then, a pretty, tall, brown haired gal came a walking out of a bedroom, and Marianne said, "Josie, meet Brave Bear's friend Red Eagle."

We told the girls, as we were eating, about our working in Montana, and a lot of small talk, and that we were kinda on our way headed back home, but decided to swing through the Black Hills on the way. Josie said there was a dance that night over at the community hall, "If you boys want us to teach you to dance, we could go over there." It didn't take me and Brave Bear long to learn how to dance a little better, and pretty soon the band was playing the last waltz.

Marianne said, "I forgot to tell you boys that the hotel in town closes at ten o'clock and won't let anyone in after that. You'll have to share our spare room or sleep in the livery barn tonight." That spare room sounded fine to us and we headed back to their house, but when we got inside the house, Marianne and Brave Bear went in that spare room and locked the door behind them.

Josie said, "Well, Red Eagle, you'll have to sleep at the foot of my bed!"

"Don't mind if I do!" That offer sure beat sleeping in the livery stable.

It had quit snowing the next morning and Marianne and Josie said they had to do some shows over at Deadwood and Sturgis, so we all headed over that way. The girls could ride as good as most men and they made me and Brave Bear ride to keep up. When we got to Deadwood, I found out it was a Wild West show and the girls and Brave Bear had been working at it before. Josie and Marianne had rooms over the old Number 10 Saloon and invited us to stay with them. We didn't take much coaxing. Brave Bear introduced me to the boss of the show, Bill Cody, and then said, "Bob, you just as well put on a breechcloth and ride around with us shooting them balloons flying in the air."

Bill said, "If you can hit them off a running horse, I can use you all the time." So it was, I hit every balloon I shot at, and I was in the show! It was easy enough and we got paid pretty good. But I kept a thinking of Lizzy back on our reservation and was sure getting anxious to get back home. Josie was a nice gal, and I could put my boots under her bed anytime, but she just wasn't Lizzy.

After, about six weeks of "Wild Westing," I told Brave Bear that Bill had asked if we would stay on and go over to Europe in the fall, but I told him I had to go home first and maybe if we weren't in jail, we might come back. "So, I'm heading home tomorrow—you want to come with me?" I asked.

"You bet," he said, "Let's go see if that offer on our pie is still good." I kinda laughed at that and said I don't know about the pie but I bet Kittie and Lora are. That got a laugh out of him too. Brave Bear said, "As long as we're leaving in the morning, I'd like to go over to the Gold Dust Saloon and see if you can win my money back from the last time I was there when they said I cheated and locked me up. They won't let me play, but you can, and I can make sure it's a fair game. I think you can win if they don't cheat!"

"Do I have a choice?" I groaned out.

"Sure," Brave Bear said, "but if you don't go, I'll go by myself anyway."

"In that case," I said, "I guess I'd better go along and try to keep you from winding up in jail again."

It was a busy bar and as soon as we were inside, Brave Bear said, "That table in the back is the one and that guy with the coat on is the one that kept pulling cards out of his sleeve."

There was an empty chair at the table, so I just worked my way back to it and sat down. "You boys mind a new player here?"

The one with the coat on said, "As long as you got money, be our guest."

We played a few hands, and I was just holding my own, when Brave Bear slid a chair up between me and the fellow with the coat on and said, "Let's make sure it's an honest game." Then he told the fellow with the coat, "You just slide that coat off and roll up them shirt sleeves." The fellow acted almost like he was going for a gun but I soon seen why he didn't—there already was a Colt tapping him on the leg and pointed right at his midsection. The coat was removed and we proceeded with our game, and it did change my luck.

I was gaining quite a bit and was wondering just how much I needed to win for Brave Bear to break even, when he tapped me on the arm, and said, "Why don't you bet your whole pile on the next hand and win, lose, or draw, we'll get out of here." And he said it plenty loud enough for the other players to hear, so I just bet it all—close to $500—before I even looked at my cards, and I came up with a hell of a good hand—four kings. It was the winning hand and we had over $1,000. I grabbed the money and headed for the door. Brave Bear backed out of the bar. He had put up his pistol, but was ready to draw if need be. No one seemed to feel like testing their luck.

As soon as we were outside, we sure didn't waste any time getting back to our "boarding house," and Marianne and Josie were both plenty happy to see us. Marianne said, "Glad you made it back out of there. I was afraid you would both get in trouble like Brave Bear did the last time he was in that bar."

"We got my money back, but I doubt if we'll ever be welcome there again!" Brave Bear said. I handed Brave Bear the money. He folded about half of it and shoved it in his vest pocket. He gave me back the rest, and said, "Keep it. I couldn't have done it alone without shooting that SOB, and I only lost about $300, the first time, anyway."

The next morning, we bid the girls good-bye, and headed home, by way of the Crow Reservation. Brave Bear said he had to go back around that way to pick up a couple extra horses that he had acquired from the Crow people. He was always trading horses and usually came out ahead of the game. But I wondered if he just didn't want to see an Indian gal there before we went on home, or maybe he didn't want to go through that Chance area again. At any rate, we headed for Rosebud, Montana, and I was sure glad to be leaving Deadwood and those gamblers behind. I really was expecting trouble somewhere along the way but we didn't have anyone following us, and by the time we got to the Montana line I felt a lot safer.

We were welcomed like old friends by the folks we knew on the Crow Reservation, but I, for one, was sure getting anxious to get home. After three days of resting with the people there, Brave Bear said, "Let's head for home first light in the morning."

"I was ready to go home even before we got here!" I said. I had the horses saddled and was tying our bedrolls and supplies on the extra horses, when Brave Bear came out and we hit the trail for home.

We were sitting by our campfire along the Powder River, when Brave Bear said, "You know, I didn't tell you why I was in a hurry to leave but was just thinking about it. I'd been over at Morristown and stopped by Jay Penney's to see if they could use some meat.

Earlier I shot a deer and hung it in a tree just south of town—figured Jay could go out with his buggy and get it. I knew Jay wasn't much on hunting. I think it was too much like work and he seemed dead set against working. Anyway, I was telling his wife, Sophie, about the deer when a bee somehow flew down the front of her dress. I suppose one came in when I did, anyway, she jerked the front on her dress open clear to her waist, and I was helping her look for that bee, when in stepped Jay and said, 'What the hell is going on?' He grabbed his rifle from over the door and said, 'I'll kill you for that, you SOB.' I was one scared bear. He had me dead cold and was about to squeeze the trigger and I knew he was too close to miss. Even if I dived to the floor and drew my pistol, he still had me. The only thing that saved me was Sophie stepped between us and pushed the barrel aside, but when she did, it went off just missing both of us.

"'Jay, you stupid fool!' Sophie hollered, 'Look at these welts on my belly! A bee was down my dress and I jerked my dress open and we were trying to get it out when you came in, and that's the God's truth.' Then she pulled up a bee still alive and kicking.

"I said, 'I've had enough of this, I'm getting out of here!' and I dived for the door. As I was half out, I turned, and hit Jay as hard as I could along side of the head. I hotfooted it to my horse and was out of town before anyone could say hey didley damn. I knew Jay couldn't catch me but he may have charged me with assault and had the town sheriff come looking for me. I might someday get shot by a jealous husband, but if I do, I at least want to be guilty!"

I just had to chuckle at his story. I knew it had to be true, but knowing Jay and Sophie made it even funnier. Sophie was a big woman, with very big breasts and not the kind of woman I could imagine Brave Bear to be fooling around with. I had never known him to even look at a married woman (there were always plenty of single gals ready and willing to chase him), and Jay was a big, easy-going guy. You'd think he wouldn't have a jealous bone in his whole body.

"That's a funny story!" I said.

"Maybe now," Brave Bear said, "but it wasn't when it was happening."

"Jay's probably cooled off some by now, but just in case, I can go over to Morristown with you when we get back," I offered.

"No, that won't be necessary! No one will ever catch me in their house again!" Brave Bear said with that very determined look of his.

As we rode on, I could hear a distant voice but couldn't make it out. Brave Bear heard it too. "Sounds like someone talking down river a ways—let's check it out!" We walked only a hundred yards down river, about halfway around a bend in the river, and there sat a Chinese boy, maybe fifteen or so, just a talking to himself in Chinese.

When he seen us, at first he looked really scared and startled, but then he said, "Samie, think you men who cut Samie's hair, but you no them!" We could see he had his hair chopped off at the neckline, and I knew, from talking with the cooks back at Noote's camp, that the Chinese believed, if they cut their hair, then they could never go back to their homeland. It was a very shameful thing to do. "Samie spit in face, then run, but they say they kill Samie! They in town that way," Samie said, and he pointed towards the next town to the east (which would be Baker, Montana).

I told him we were heading that way in the morning. Maybe he should go back with us and we could get his "pigtail" back for him.

"No! No! They verwe mean men, they kill Samie!" he said.

"Some things aren't always as they seem. Maybe they aren't so mean and I don't think they can kill Samie," Brave Bear said.

I said, "Let's get on back to our campfire, and see if Samie can eat something!"

"Samie no money, but Samie cook!" he explained.

We already had coffee and beans a cooking, but I said fine. Samie ate enough to feed three growing boys, but I figured he probably hadn't eaten a meal in quite a while, and he had just been running close to twenty miles so he had to of worked up a big appetite. In the morning, I woke up to the smell of fresh coffee. Samie was up and had the fire a going and had made some coffee, and Brave Bear was gathering in the horses (we had them hobbled so they didn't go far). We saddled up and put our gear and bedrolls on just one horse. I used a halter on my horse and put my bridle on the extra horse and handed the reins to Samie.

Brave Bear said to Samie, "Get on, you'll have to ride bareback until we get to town and find you a saddle."

Samie said, "No can wride horsey."

Brave Bear just grabbed him under the arms and swung him up on the horse and handed him the reins and said, "You no learn any younger!"

We were about halfway to Baker when we seen three riders coming in our direction, and as we got closer to them, Samie said something in Chinese, then said, "Them men, chop chop, Samie hair!"

Brave Bear said, "Samie, you just hang back a little and if them boys get past me and Bob, why you just ride like hell for China." When those boys were about twenty feet in front of us, Brave Bear turned his horse to the left. He was broadside of them with his right hand on his Colt, so I just turned my horse to the right and rested my hand on my Colt. (I was left-handed so it was the good position for me if I needed to draw fast.) The boys stopped short and I thought, they don't look so tough.

Brave Bear said, in a loud voice, "You boys have something that belongs to a friend of ours and we will just have it back, and right pronto-like too!"

They evidently didn't feel lucky enough to try to draw. One of them said, "We don't want trouble from you. We was just having some fun." They were looking at Samie, so they knew exactly what Brave Bear was talking about. "If it means that much to you guys, here." He reached into his saddlebag and pulled out Samie's braid (he must've kept it for a souvenir) and threw it on the ground in front of his horse.

"That won't do!" Brave Bear said. "You boys owe our friend an apology. Just slip them gun belts off now and slide out of them saddles. You've insulted a man, and you either apologize proper or, by God, you'd better be ready to fight like hell! I doubt if you boys are big enough to do either, but we'll let Samie decide."

One of the guys said, "We gave back his hair, and that's all the apology he's going to get from us!" They did drop their gun belts and dismounted so Brave Bear and I got off our horses too, and by now Samie was right up alongside of Brave Bear.

Samie joined in and said, "You hold, Samie chop chop!" Them boys didn't like them words and they came diving at us. Well, that was the wrong thing to do. I caught the one nearest me with a right, then a hard left. His legs buckled and he went down and out. Brave Bear connected with the second one and put a neck lock on the third guy. Samie was on the one I had sent to the ground and had a handful of pants and a very sharp knife that he had came up with from somewhere. Chop-chop and he had a handful of trousers crotch and two testicles. Like a cat, he was on the other one that Brave Bear had knocked down and same results. Then he reached in from behind Brave Bear and de-jeweled that fellow too. We had Samie's apology in less than a minute.

Brave Bear threw Samie on his horse, and said, "We best be a fanning the breeze out of here." Then he said to the three guys groaning on the ground, "We're heading into Indian Territory and if you boys come a looking for Samie there, you'll likely get scalped!"

It didn't take us long to get to Baker and pick up a saddle and a bridle for Samie, and head on to North Dakota. We had been riding for two days now, and we were about to make it home for supper. Thunder Hawk was in sight and we still had plenty of daylight. We stopped at Bamble's Store in Thunder Hawk, and Samie got a job right away, cleaning and stocking shelves for Mr. Bamble. I was sure he would. Mr. Bamble usually needed help, and there was a spare room above the store for Samie so he was set.

Brave Bear said, "Samie, you just keep that horse, just in case you need to ride somewhere!"

Samie said, "No, no—no money!"

Brave Bear just grinned at Samie, tipped his hat, and we headed home.

Mother would be cooking supper about now. Dad was just heading to the house when he seen us come a riding in. He looked surprised at first but came right over and shook our hands and even gave me a hug. I hadn't had a hug from my dad in at least ten years! Then he said, "Here let me put up your horses, you boys get on in and wash up for supper." Mother was at the stove when I stepped through the door but she gave me the longest hug and Brave Bear got one too. Jimmie came running over and hugged me around the legs, and Bessie came and gave a hug and a peck on the check.

"Wow, you two have sure been a growing while I was gone," I said to Jimmie, "I've got a job for you. I ordered a new saddle out at Miles City from Hamlin Saddlery, and they said they'd ship it to Thunder Hawk when they have it made. I want you to break it in for me when it gets here!" Jimmie was all smiles with that and said he'd take care of it real good, too. Jimmie liked that saddle so much, I never did get to even use it.

"Oh it is so good to have my boys back," Mother said, reaching for a pan on the stove, "I had better get back to my cooking though or we'll have burnt supper."

Dad came in shortly, and appraised us closely, "Don't look like you boys are too much the worst for the wear. They must have fed you all right!"

"Out in Montana we had real cooks—Chinamen—and they were plenty good too." I told them that some Chinamen had quit the railroad when they were building tracks through Montana and went to work for Noote and Pete, and the Chinamen were still cooking there now, except for one that bled to death.

"Let's hear all about Montana," Dad said.

"There isn't much to tell," said Brave Bear. "A cowhand there is about the same as here, and we couldn't drink in town 'cause they don't serve Indians there either, so we stayed out of trouble and got paid good for the work."

Then I started, "We didn't even get to work together. I worked on the north ranch and Brave Bear was on the south one so it was a dang boring job. Some of the hands rushed to get through chores and run back to the bunkhouse to play cards, but Brave Bear kept winning all their money so after the second month they wouldn't play with him. And the ones at my bunkhouse mostly played pinochle. I wouldn't learn how to play it, so I did a lot of reading and, usually, a lot of extra observing."

After the best dinner any cowhand ever had—thick steaks with all the trimmings—Mother reached into her skirt pocket and pulled out two envelopes. "Your father said these were for you," she said, handing one to me and one to Brave Bear. They had our names "in care of Ben Gilland" written on them and were postmarked from Miles City, Montana. Inside each was a bank draft for $1,100 and an itemized note saying,

> $450—seven and one-half months' wages,
> $150—reward for five cattle rustlers, and
> $500—bonus.
> from Noote & Pete
>
> P.S. You boys have an open invite to a job anytime you want to come on back, as long as we own this ranch. You did a great job.
> Our Thanks,
> Noote & Pete
>
> P.P.S. That sheriff at Sheridan is doing time in his jail. He was taking a payoff from those rustlers.
> Noote & Pete

I just signed my check and handed it to Dad, "Here's part of the money I owe you."

Brave Bear signed his and handed it to Dad too, and said, "Ben, will you put this in the bank for me?"

Dad said that of course he would, first thing it the morning. I had over $1,000 from my regular wages and my "gambling winnings" I had collected over the past year, so I pulled out my money from my inner vest pocket and counted out $900. I put the rest back in my pocket (I had to have some to spend foolishly). I handed Dad the $900, and said, "Well, this should cover that $1,750 loan. If it's close enough for you, it's fine with me. Thanks for being so good about it." Dad was speechless and looked like he couldn't believe I had got that much money together.

Mother seemed curious about the note so I handed it to her (she would have Dad or Bessie read it to her later). She said, "I think I'll head upstairs to bed."

"You staying the night, Brave Bear?" I asked.

"No," he said, "it's still pretty early. I think I'll just ride on over to Ed Hodgekinson's for the night. It's only a few miles, and he always stays up late and sleeps in the mornings so I'd best go tonight."

Mother said, "You are sure welcome to stay here."

"I know, but I haven't seen Ed in a long while either." And with a thanks for supper he headed out the door.

Mother had a smile on her face so I asked her to tell us what she knew that she wasn't telling us.

"Oh," she said, "It's probably not funny, but I'd like to see the look on Brave Bear's face when he gets over to Ed's and finds out that Emma and Louise got married. The only girl around Ed's place now is Agnes, and she's younger than Jimmie who's just seven."

The next morning I asked Dad if he would kind of keep an eye on a Chinese boy who had rode back with us from up around Baker and took a job at Bamble's store. I said, "Samie doesn't speak good English, and he has some different ways about him, than some around here, but I think he's a good fellow and doesn't deserve to be picked on!" "He'll be treated fair in Thunder Hawk. I'll see to that!" Dad said.

CHAPTER II

Shopping at the Glad Valley Store

Right after breakfast, I headed south to help Ben and check over my homestead. Dad had Abe and Ben breaking horses and he had said that I just as well go help them for a couple of months, 'til those cattle the Agency was giving out were ready to be picked up at Fort Yates. As I was riding along, a lot of thoughts crossed my mind, mostly of Lizzy and what she had been doing for the past eight months. Maybe she didn't wait, maybe her and Alice both got married like the Hodgekinson girls. Well, I'd be finding out very shortly.

I wondered how that homesteader Howard Ennerson was getting along with my horse that I had traded him last spring. I had ridden over to his place last spring on my way back from checking Dad's cattle over on Thunder Hawk Creek, about ten or twelve miles from home. He had a well-matched team—a four- and a five-year old—in the corral and offered to trade them to me for my saddle horse. I knew that well-matched team would be worth a lot more than my saddle horse once they were broke, but they weren't broke—just halter broke. Anyway, I traded him a horse for two horses. I saddled up one of them and they were real gentle, so I led them out of the corral and tied the other one to the tail of the first one, and swung onto the saddled one. Boy did I get a ride. The first tried bucking, but every time he did the second one pulled back and that kept up for a mile or so; finally, the lead one quit trying to pitch me off and we went on home.

My house was just the way I had left it, but sure was a lot of dust settled on everything. Maybe I'd just go on over to Ben's. He should be in for lunch by the time I get over there. Ben and Abe were just walking towards the house when I rode up, and they both were happy to see me.

"Come on, I was just going in to throw on some grub, then we can take a couple of them green teams for a spin," Ben said. I hoped he didn't mean that literally—a team spinning around isn't much fun and a good way to bust the reach out of the wagon, and then let the excitement begin. I had done that once already. Dad always said that too much weight will break the wagon tongue, and a broken tongue in a hitched wagon is worse than a broken reach.

"I'll take the lead with my team and you just follow. Abe can ride along as an outrider with his bronc, and maybe give us a hand if our horses get to acting up," he offered. I wasn't sure where Ben was heading, but he turned toward the southeast and by the time we had gone past Black Horse Butte, I had a pretty good idea where I was going, even if he turned around and went back home. Ben's team seemed to be picking up steam now and he was getting ahead of me a ways and out of hearing distance.

Abe was riding next to me, so I asked, "Abe, what happened with Ben and Maude? Ben would never go with me over to Archambault's before and now he's leading me right over there."

Abe replied, "The scuttlebutt has it that Maude got knocked up and she'd been seeing an Art Phillips too. Ben wasn't sure if it was his and was dragging his feet about marrying her, so she up an married Art. That was last fall and he's been hard to live around all winter, but he took Alice home from a dance over at the Grand Valley Hall a month ago and made several trips over there lately to help Old Louie." Louie Jr. was on a colt in the corral when we drove up and Abe rode right over and started talking with him. Ben and

I were just tying our teams to the corral rails when two gals came a running out of the Archambault house.

I met Lizzy and she just jumped into my arms. We kissed a long kiss and hugged even longer, then she said, "Oh, I thought you were never coming back."

"I had to make enough money to pay Dad back and I did. But I don't have any plans on leaving again. You're prettier than ever and I think I'll just take you home with me." She was all smiles and blushed a little but seemed to sparkle with that idea.

"Only say what you mean, but I would go, if that's a proposal," she said. We just looked at each other but I knew she meant it too.

Ben interrupted our silence, "I've got an idea. Why don't you hire the girls to come back with us to clean up your house? They can stay there tonight and you can stay with me, and we can bring them back tomorrow. Abe can stay over here with Junior. Louie and Maria and the other kids went over to Fort Yates this morning and won't be back for a couple of days!"

I looked at Lizzy and agreed that I could even pay each of the girls $10 and stay out of their way while they cleaned. Lizzy said, "Let's go, but you don't have to pay us and it won't be any fun if you stay out of my way."

"I'll ride back a ways with you guys and pony Junior's colt along for him," Abe said. "Every time Junior tries riding outside of the corral his horse goes to bucking like a scolded dog." When we got about halfway home Abe said that he and Junior were going to head back. He told Junior, "I'm turning you lose—that colt should be tired enough now to go without bucking." They rode off and it looked like Abe was right. When we got to Ben's, he said, "You go on, we'll be up to your place in a little."

That was fine with me, and Lizzy didn't seem to mind either. She went right to cleaning and dusting and kept me busy bringing in wood and fetching water. Then she said, "I'll fix us supper if you will go shoot us a grouse or rabbit."

"I won't have to do that, there's a lot of canned meat and vegetables out in the root cellar." Since the folks didn't know when I'd be back, they always made sure there was plenty of food in the cellar.

"I don't like going in cellars, but if you will bring in something I'll cook whatever you bring in." So I gathered up a few spuds and a jar of beef and jar of green beans and by the time I got back into the house she was already mixing up a batch of biscuits. After she had stuff in pots on the stove and the biscuits in the oven, she said, "Now what! We'll just have to wait twenty minutes or so for the spuds and biscuits to get done. What's a girl to do?" And she went over and lay on the bed, and said, "I think I'll just rest 'til the food is done. Bob, you can do whatever you want." I thought, maybe a little rest would do me some good too.

Ben and Alice never did show up, but after breakfast Lizzy and I headed back, and when we got to Ben's, they were already buggied up and coming out to the main trail, so we just waved and headed on out for Louie's place. Lizzy was beaming to talk now and she told about how poor they were and how it really helped out when we had left money under our plates, and that there was a social at Grand Valley Hall and now that I was back she would like to go if only I would ask to take her.

"It'd be my pleasure," I said, but I hadn't even known about it. "You know, I just got back and I haven't had time to catch up of the goings on around here, but anytime you want to do something just say so. I'd take you to the end of the world if you ask me to." She said she hoped her folks got back early (her mother had promised to try to buy some material for making a new dress and she hoped there would be enough time to get one made for the social. When we got to Louie's place, I said to Ben and Alice, "Hey let's go on over to the Glad Valley General Store; I want to buy a new dress." This took Ben and Alice by surprise; even Lizzy had a look on her face like someone had just pinched her on the butt.

"Come on, we just as well all go in one buggy!" Ben said.

When we got in the store, Lizzy said in a teasing way, "I suppose you're getting a dress for your mother. Do you want me to model it for you?"

"Sure," I said, "I think Mother likes pink." Lizzy knew what I meant; she'd put a pink ribbon on her basket and had on a well-worn pink dress at the previous pie social. She picked out a pretty pink dress and hurried to the back room to try it on. When she came out modeling it, she was just as pretty as a picture.

"I wonder if that store keep can find a set of earrings and a necklace that would match," I said. The storekeeper heard me, and right away pulled out his jewelry from under the counter and sure enough, had just the match. "What about shoes?" I said. There wasn't any pink ones, but a pair of black ones fit Lizzy just fine.

"Oh no, that's too much, I couldn't take them too!"

"Why not?" I said with a mock frown, "They match, they sure are pretty on you, and Mother should really like them."

Lizzy just laughed, and whispered in my ear, "I'll marry you in them then! Then she said, "Well if I'm going in new clothes you are too," and she waltzed over to the men's shirts and started looking through them.

"Fine," I said, "but I don't think I'd look right in a pink one." Ben was in a dilemma with Alice; she had modeled a red dress and a blue one and was modeling a brown one, and asked him which one he liked best. When she went to take off the brown dress I said to Ben, "It's your choice, but I'm sure she likes red the best," and it was Ben's choice too. Just as soon as she returned, red it was. Ben wouldn't be outdone so Alice had a new pair of shoes too, and earrings and a necklace.

We had two of the prettiest women at the pie social at Grand Valley, and they didn't mix up the baskets this time. But Brave Bear didn't show up, and I couldn't help but wonder what he was up to, and what he would think of Ben sparking Alice. Brave Bear and Ben were good friends and Brave Bear didn't have a ring on Alice's finger so there shouldn't be a problem between them. And besides, Brave Bear very likely was with a woman, wherever he was. But he never seemed to get attached to any certain one, like some do.

CHAPTER 12

Trailing the Herd to Thunder Hawk

We had been picking up riders all the way from Thunder Hawk to help herd the cattle the Agency was giving out to Indian ranchers. Fort Yates was a bustling when we got there—horses, buggies, and wagons were pulled up everywhere. People were going in and out the Agency offices and the stores were all crowded. We had signed all the paperwork close to a month ago and had a letter from the Agency stating that we were to pick up our cattle at the mouth of Porcupine Creek, the last Monday of July, and today just happened to be that day. By signing the paperwork, each rancher was allotted twenty-five head and agreed to give the tribe back a heifer sometime down the road for each one he took.

The more than two thousand Herefords branded for their seventy-nine different new owners was supposed to be waiting for us about a five-mile ride away down on Porcupine Creek. The cattle had been branded "ID" for Indian Department on the right hip and each person getting cattle was assigned an individual brand number. The boys branding the ID also put the brands on each twenty-five head, that way no one got to pick their cattle. My brand was 222 on the right ribs and Ben's was 121 on the right ribs.

The cattle that were to go north had already been taken that way. Those for Louie Archambault and the rest of the ranchers—and would-be ranchers—south and west were being held just a few miles south of Fort Yates.

Now we were about to gather up the herd and head on west trailing them across the prairie past Chadwick's, then along the Cannon Ball River 'til we hit the Cedar River, then we would trail along the Cedar and head for Thunder Hawk. When we got close to Thunder Hawk, Ben and I would head south to the Grand River with our cattle. Ben and I had met up with most of the boys from around Thunder Hawk—Tom Powers, Charlie Hodgekinson, Levi and Ernie Wagner, Ben Irons, Pete Dempsey, Arthur Vermillion, Ace Kempton, Charles Hourigan, Hank Ploog, Felix Fly, Roy Flying Horse, and Bob Bobtail Blue Bear. Several white men that had married Indian women were there to pick up cattle too—Gene Benson, Turkey Track Bill Malush, and quite a few others. We had made it to Fort Yates in a long day but going back to Thunder Hawk would take more like ten days.

We spread our bedrolls that night on the old powwow grounds by the Agency headquarters building, but we slept restless, ready to get our cattle and get back to Thunder Hawk. The dry lightning arching across the sky and my thoughts of Lizzy didn't help my sleeping much. It was just breaking daylight, and it was getting light enough to see quite a ways around us as we rode down the south slope of Porcupine Creek. We should be right about in the middle of a bunch of cattle, but there wasn't a cow to be seen anywhere.

Ben looked mad as a wet hen over at me and said, "I told you to get the lead out or we were going to be late. They already left without us!" A half a dozen riders were up ahead of us a hundred yards or so just sitting on their horses, and more like twenty or more straggled along behind us. The ones in front were Gene, Ace, Charlie Hodgekinson, Levi and Ernie Wagner, and Charles Hourigan—our group from Thunder Hawk. As we rode up, Ben spoke first, "Where's the cattle?

Gene was quick to answer back, "We have been asking ourselves that same question, but no one seems to know. We got here when it was still dark and there weren't no cattle here then neither."

I said, talking like I was a real authority on the subject, "Most likely the cattle bolted last night. Lightning and thunder has been known to spook many a herd, causing them to stampede." I was thinking that the night crew last night—mostly fellows like Tom, Arthur, and Hank who didn't have much experience herding more than a couple of milk cows—probably couldn't hold the cattle, or maybe they didn't like sitting out here in the rain in a thunderstorm, and just let the cattle go. I thought it but instead of saying it, I settled for some hard looks at those boys. Out loud I said, "Let's ride over west a few miles 'til we get up on one of those high hills and maybe we can see cattle or run into someone who knows something anyway."

Gene was quick to respond to my comments, "Let's do'er." And we were off. The rest all came right along too, even the stragglers. Some of them were a bouncing and bobbing around a lot on their horses, but they were sure trying to catch up with the crowd. I kept looking back at those "cowboys" a bouncing around of their horses and I got to thinking, I bet some of them haven't rode a horse much. There will sure be some cowboys with blisters on their legs and rear ends by the time we make camp tonight!

As soon as we reached the highest hill to the west, the one we were heading for, we could see the cattle. Over to the east side of the Porcupine Hills, about fifteen miles away, we could see cattle in a bunch being held by riders just about where we were supposed to meet up with our wagon boss. Ace's uncle, Casper Kempton, had agreed to bring his team and wagon and cook for our crew from Thunder Hawk. We each had to pay him one buck a day for the meals and we could throw our bedrolls on his wagon. Casper had cooked for several big outfits at different roundups and he was good at his job. Seeing the wagon reminded me that we didn't yet have breakfast today. I had some jerky and dried stuff in my saddlebags and right about pretty soon would be a good time to make use of my stash.

Some riders were chasing cattle west about five miles ahead of us and more riders were gathering up cattle to the south a few miles. There were cattle scattered clear north almost to Porcupine Creek and a few riders were gathering in cattle from over that way too.

"Guess we know where the cattle went!" Gene said loudly,

Ben came back with, under his breath like he was just talking to himself, "Wonder how many were lost in the stampede? Good thing some of the hands here know how to run cattle."

"Looks like we could help in about three different directions," Ernie grumbled in his usual deep voice.

Gene summed it up for us, "The boys in the middle look like they are getting along the best, so let's us experienced riders split and go north and south." Looking back over his shoulder at Tom and some of the others, he said, "Let those *wanobish wa-ceen-un* (want-to-be's) catch up with those in front of us." We were off! By noon, we had the cattle back in a pretty loose herd and there wasn't much run left in them. Now they were about as hard to move as a bunch of old woolies. Casper was all set up and ready to feed us and some of us were quite a bit more than hungry. The plan had come together and didn't take long either.

Turkey Track Bill had came into this country with a big cattle company from Texas, so he had a lot of experience with trailing cattle herds and was in charge of the head count. The Agency had given him the job of making sure each person got exactly his twenty-five head. He'd stayed with Casper at the wagon so he was the one that got out front of the cattle and got them circled and stopped the stampede. But they got in a long run anyway before they got stopped and there were a few dead ones along the way. The Agency had sorted in an extra hundred head the day before, just in case some didn't make the drive. If any rancher couldn't find his branded twenty-five head, he could take some of the extras to make up his count. The Gayton place was just to the south of where we were and Silks lived just to east of them and they ran their cattle together, so they were the first to get their cattle. There were four different brands among the family members, but they could all be in one sort.

Turkey Track bellowed, "Boys! I want some of you to hold the cattle and some to help sort. You Gilland boys, Ace, Gene, Ben Irons, and Jim Murphy, help me sort out the herd. Gayton and Silk, you hold your cattle back a ways from the herd and when we get your head count, just get behind your cattle and get them out of here. Hourigan and Hodgekinson, take up a position between the herd and the sort and keep count. The rest of you, position yourselves around the herd and keep them from drifting but let them spread out enough so we can sort without running over cattle. Don't get in the way of the sorters." He read off the four brands to start looking for and said, "Any questions?" No one said anything, and after about a minute, he said, "Good then, let's get at it," as he swung up on his horse and everyone else followed suit.

Ben and I had plenty of practice at sorting cattle and we knew the slower we went about it the faster we would get the job done. We tried working out as many at a time as we could. By working together with the other sorters, when we each worked one critter over to the edge, chances were good that we could work out several in a little group. It was a lot faster and easier to get four of twelve to head out away from the bunch than it was to chase just one at a time. We had our first hundred sorted off in less than an hour and we went right at sorting off more to go north, but those boys ran separate herds and wanted to take their sort in their separate little groups. Didn't matter to us but we sorted off fifty for Gipps and they headed north and we sorted twenty-five for Comeau and he headed his north too.

Before we finished getting Dunn's seventy-five head out of the herd, we could see up to the north a mile or so, Comeau's herd was really gaining on Gipp's bunch. Soon, we could hear a lot of distant yelling and Comeau's cattle were zipping past the Gipp riders and were totally mixed up in very short order. Too bad, but we had did our part at getting them sorted in the first place. We'd gotten rid of about a third of the herd and it was beginning to feel like a long day when Turkey Track shouted out, "That's it for today. Get rested up. We'll take shifts herding from now until first light, then we'll try to make it over to Chadwick's by tomorrow night. There's a four-wire fenced-in holding pasture there and it takes in Porcupine Creek so everyone will get a good night's sleep tomorrow night. We may hold over there an extra day and let these heifers get a little rest up too.

It was a cool morning with a northwest breeze so the cattle should travel good today and it was time to be a moving them out.

Turkey Track rode out towards the herd and bellowed, "Get em up and head em northwest." We went north of the Porcupine Hills and kept the cattle on mostly level ground and they moved right along. We were pushing the last ones through the gate at Chadwick's with a couple of hours of daylight to spare.

We were about five miles from the settlement at Porcupine and the Goudreau boys lived right close to the settlement. Brave Bear and I stayed with them last year when we cut horses here at Chadwick's. Bunky Goudreau asked lightly, "Bob, do you want to go home with us for a home-cooked meal and a warm bed?"

It sure was tempting, but in the back of my mind I knew Lizzy wouldn't be much in favor of me spending the night there, so I said, "No, think I'll just hang around camp and give Casper a hand, but Ben might take the offer."

Ben eagerly said, "Sure," then he added, "I have been batching it all year and I'm not going to pass on an offer like that."

As they were riding out, I hollered at them, "Try to get back here in time to help sort cattle in the morning!"

We were well into sorting cattle before Ben, Snooky, and Bunky showed up, but they were stone sober and looked like they did get a good night's sleep. I did catch Ben rubbing his eyes for some reason, but I didn't pry; figured, best leave well enough alone. By noon, we were noticeably shorter on cattle. When we stopped for lunch, Turkey Track said, "Boys, we've cut out seven hundred cattle and only have the Goudreau's to sort this afternoon, so we don't have to get in a big rush. Some of our horses could use a rest anyway."

Tomorrow we would head over to the Cannon Ball River and camp just south of Jim Murphy's and sort off his cattle there, and that would dwindle down the herd some more. After the sort at Murphy's we would only have around three hundred fifty head to move on west. We were losing some of our help too, but we still had plenty of riders, and some were even good hands, but for my part, Tom and Arthur could have just as well stayed at home.

The Cannon Ball River was a mere trickle now but I had seen it when it would be danged tough getting across. To stay out of the difficult creeks and some really rough badland breaks, Turkey Track had us cross the Cannon Ball just a couple miles below the mouth of the Cedar River. We stayed on the north side of the Cannon Ball for most of the day, then we crossed back and went south until we crossed the Cedar. Next we went west a ways and made camp for one more night. We were really making good time with the cattle, the weather stayed kinda cool for August, and the wind, when it was noticeable, was coming from the west and that made it easier to trail the cattle in that direction.

Next day was a different story. As we headed straight west, the Cedar River took a big bend back to the north and west so it looked a lot shorter just going across country. Well, it wasn't taking into account that there was thorn bushes, hawthorns, plum thickets, buffalo berry bushes, and scrub trees growing in every low spot and on every little hillside. The cattle just loved sashaying under them bushes—it was getting hot and the bushes made good shade. The cows brushed flies off their backs by walking under the thorn bushes, but it was sure tough on horses and riders trying to get through. Most of us were wearing chaps, but still it was darn near impossible riding a horse through all them bushes.

Turkey Track Bill had experience with this kind of country before. He yelled out, "Half you whippersnappers get off your horses and act like a bunch of barking dogs. Tom, Hank, Arthur, give your reins to Ben and Bob. You Gilland boys bring their horses around the other side of these bushes." That did work to some degree, but it sure made for a lot of walking, and cowboys—even the ones who weren't much account on the trail—just weren't much on walking. The boys groused at Turkey Track Bill but he just turned a deaf ear. "Real dogs would have worked better," he said kinda to himself, "and they don't complain neither." But we had orders to shoot any dogs that were within seeing distance of the herd because dogs had been known to get to chasing cattle and run cattle plumb to death.

Ben came a riding over about the time we had the cattle headed out on a clear stretch again. Looking at his pocket watch, he said in a very dry voice tinted with a bit of sarcasm, "We started the cattle out at a little before seven this morning and it's now one o'clock, so we have really been making good time, almost a half a mile an hour."

I came back with, "Well, as hot as it's getting, if we keep chasing these cattle, we'll all be dropping over with a heat stroke." The cattle were headed for a little creek that had trees around on both sides and a spring-fed water hole; some of the cattle were already diving into the water.

Turkey Track yelled, "Let those doggies go, and gather around." That was his way of explaining his plans for the operation. "It's close to a hundred degrees and getting hotter. The cattle can't be chased in this heat and they won't leave that spot 'til it starts cooling down. Let's just go on up ahead to the river and chuck wagon. And after you've ate, some of you boys just grab old Casper and haul him right over to the river and throw him in. I don't think he's had time to take a bath lately and he probably needs one. I know the rest of us do. He didn't get an argument from any of us; we just headed for camp.

Casper had a big meal laid out for us, and I for one wasn't going to throw him in the river. I respected him too much for that. I was pondering it over in my mind as to what do if the boys tried grabbing Casper, and I was leaning to the idea of helping the old man. When we had all finished eating, Casper got up and instead of preparing to wash pots and pans, he just started walking towards the river bank with several bars of lye soap in his hands. Without a word, he nodded at the boys that had circled around Turkey Track. Off to the river they all went with Turkey Track hoisted into the air and then into the river kersplash! Casper laid the soap on the bank and stripped off and jumped in and started scrubbing down with the soap, by now everyone was lined out along the riverbank and shedding clothes. Turkey Track managed to get back out of the river and was getting out of his wet clothes. It was at least a hundred degrees, and getting hotter, so it wouldn't take long for wet clothes to dry if they were hung over the bushes. Turkey Track took the dousing good-naturedly—it was his idea in the first place. The water was a tad bit cold but sure was refreshing. There were a lot of springs along the Cedar that kept it running most of the time and kept it cold too.

Along the banks of the Grand River. Photo by Frank Bennett Fiske used with permission of the State Historical Society of North Dakota.

We swam and splashed around in the river for the better part of the afternoon, and we were kinda looking for something else to do. Ben found it—anyway he spotted it first—a big fish trying to swim upstream was stuck in the rocks at a ripple in the bend of the river just to the west of where we were swimming. We must have spooked it out of the deep water and it couldn't quite make it over the rocks in shallow water. Ben grabbed up a beaver-cut stick about five feet long that was laying along the bank, and went in leaps and bounds for the fish. When he got there he whacked it really hard a crossed the head. Ben managed to work his stick through one gill and out of that big fish's mouth, but I got there just in the nick of time to pick up the other end of the stick and we went a carrying a pike fish that was over thirty pounds, back to our chuck wagon. Casper said right away, "I know just how to fillet that fish so there won't even be any bones in the meat, and there'll be enough to feed this whole crew." None of us ever seen a fish that big so that was the topic for the rest of the afternoon. And Ben got a new name, *ho-KU-wah-s'ah* (fisherman).

The next morning started out hot; it wasn't the day to move cattle very far. We did manage to get the herd a few miles more west before the heat stopped us again, but the river had taken another swing north and we were now a few miles south of the river right about on the North Dakota and South Dakota line not more than fifteen miles from Thunder Hawk. I was thinking to myself, just about one more day to tolerate Tom's bragging and his general uselessness on the trail and Arthur's peculiar silence. I had thought more than once that both my cousins could use a black eye but always managed to talk myself out of it. When we made camp at night, we had a smaller crew and not so many cattle either; Turkey Track sorted off his and Ace had taken his and his folks'. The Kemptons lived just a couple of miles to the south of where we were, Turkey Track lived a little to the north, and Ben Irons lived just to the southwest a few miles. We were going to be without a trail boss, but Gene had pretty much taken on the job and he had told Turkey Track that he would keep any extra cattle at his place until the BIA decided where to put them. We'd gotten a good count on the cattle and we were right at two head long on the count, so must have lost ninety-eight in the stampede!

Casper stayed with us though, so we still could eat pretty good. He had cooked up that big fish for us and he did a right smart job. I figured it was about the best fish I'd ever eaten, but then I hadn't eaten a lot of fish. I was thinking that we were almost to Thunder Hawk and this would likely be our last night on the trail, when Ben said to me, "I'm going to head on home for the night. I'll come back in the morning and help sort our cattle and bring you a fresh horse. We'll have to trail our cattle down south twenty miles and we'll have to push hard to make it to the Grand in one day." Then he headed off.

Gene rode over to Henry and Frank Mentz—the Mentz brothers had been hired by the BIA to assist with getting the cattle distributed, but they were more like a thorn in the rear than help on the trail—and spoke loud enough that we all heard him, "I'm going home too. Casper already has camp started, so just bed down the cattle up by his camp and I'll see all of you in the morning.

Keep an eye on the cattle," and he waved as he turned his horse north and headed home.

We had been on the trail for eight days, dropping off cattle to the different ranches and homesteads as we went along, and we were about home. In the morning, we would sort off mine and Ben's heifers and head south to the Grand River. There was a good spot to bed down the cattle just north of Quay's place, so we set up camp there and were about to roll in when along comes Ed Duncan, who had a couple of bottles of whiskey with him, and Charlie Gayton rode along with Ed to keep him company. We'd been trailing cattle all day and most of the boys hadn't bothered to take off their guns or boots yet. I'd started to put out my bedroll so my gun was under it already. Ed said that he thought we might want to celebrate a little and he passed around the bottles. Tom, Arthur, Charlie, Felix—most of the boys joined in. Dakota in August is a thirst-making place, and well, I hadn't had a drink in a long time so I figured what the hell. When you're twenty and it's summer, you just know a drink with the boys can't hurt anything. Charlie and Ed had a couple drinks, then they said they had to be getting back to McIntosh.

We were sitting around the campfire and proceeded in sipping on that whiskey and telling stories. I was telling about some of my experiences in Montana, when Tom said, "Ah, bullshit." Tom was Mother's nephew, but we hadn't gotten along ever, and he was always wanting to see how tough I was.

"Well," I said, "I'll just go ride out and check the cattle then," feeling some of that whiskey was mixing things up a bit. I jumped onto my horse but the horse wasn't where he was when I started and I'd forgotten about not having a saddle on. Tom slapped my horse hard and I slide off rearwards.

"Some big cowboy, can't even get on a horse," Tom said. But he didn't stop there. He went on with a long list of names for me and none of them were Red Eagle or Bob.

"You shouldn't a hit my horse," I said.

He laughed and whacked him again so he took off across the grass. That and the whiskey was enough to bring out the fight in me. I made a dive for Tom and we scuffled around the mess wagon.

We were both too drunk to land a good punch, but then Tom went for his gun.

I turned and rolled over toward the wagon and grabbed my revolver from out of my bedroll. The rest of the boys grabbed their guns too. Tom just laughed and said, "You yellow bastard, you don't have the guts!" He was coming fast at me. I had a choice—either shoot or run, so I shot in the air. Too much was going on too fast for much concentration but I heard shots being fired. I thought they were from Tom's gun. He kept coming so I shot again and then Tom dropped to the ground.

Everyone gathered around him then but he was dead before anyone could do anything. He had two bullet holes in him—one nicking his side and that is where I thought I aimed and another one right through the middle, and that one was the one that did him in. There were a couple bullet holes in the wagon box behind me, so someone, if not Tom, was shooting very close to me too. One bullet mark looked like it missed me by almost a half inch and the other one was near a hit.

We all just stood there trying to figure out what had happened. Each one of us was still holding his gun and there was a lot a whiskey-clouded talk and pointing going on about which bullet went where.

"Tom was aiming at right for Bob," Felix Fly stammered trying to show us with his shaky gun hand.

Karl Hourigan said, "I heard a lot of shots go off."

As usual, Arthur didn't say much, but one thing for sure—Tom was lying dead on the ground.

I figured if it was my bullet, it was self-defense, but I'd better try to catch up with Charlie Gayton and tell him what had happened. Charlie had made it back to McIntosh before I caught up with him. When I told him what had happened, he put me in a cell in his jail and said he would go check it out.

After I left to catch up with Charlie, the boys put Tom up over his horse and Arthur and Karl Hourigan headed to the Powers ranch with their heavy burden. My head pounded in that jail cell, but I never expected to hear what Charlie had to say.

When he came back he said, "Bad news for you, Bob. I'm going to have to hold you for murder." I thought turning myself in would show him that I had nothing to hide and the boys would tell the whole story. If I'd known then that the boys wouldn't even be asked to tell what they saw, I'd a been on the way to Hole-in-the-Wall.

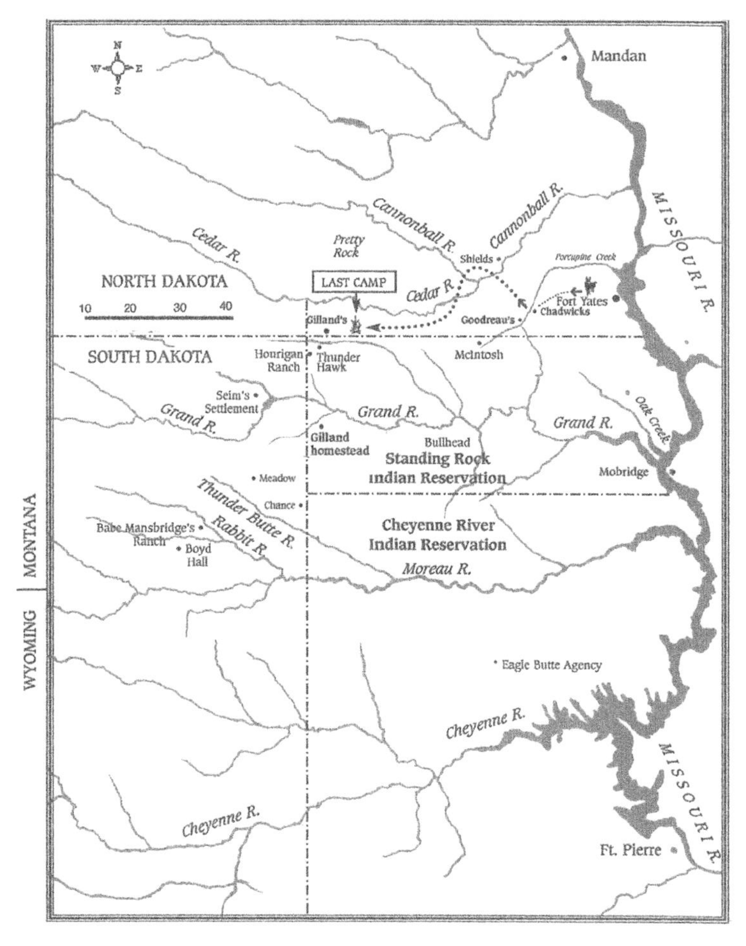

Map 3. The Last Camp on the Trail to Thunder Hawk

CHAPTER 13

Booze Thought to Be the Cause

The boys took the cattle on to Thunder Hawk. Charlie phoned Sheriff Perry at the Agency in Fort Yates to tell him what happened, and he wired me a train ticket from McIntosh to Aberdeen, South Dakota. When I got to the depot, not only was the sheriff there but also Major W. I. Belden, the Superintendant from the Standing Rock Agency. Belden brought Henry and Frank Mentz along as "witnesses." All of us were going two hundred miles away to Aberdeen where the Federal Court would be held. The federal government didn't trust the Indians' sense of justice so major crimes committed on Indian reservations were tried in Federal Court. But trials were usually held for crimes committed on the Standing Rock Reservation in Deadwood or Fort Yates. Aberdeen was a long ways from the reservation on the other side of the Missouri where I didn't know anyone and no one knew me.

The attorneys of Aberdeen, however, worked hard to get the Federal Court session to meet there. Lots of people came in to town during court sessions and spent their money. The courthouse was crowded with Indians and whites who had come to see the trials of cases against Indians or whites charged with crimes involving Indians, including offenses peculiar to laws governing the reservation, such as selling liquor. My case was first up. The twelve white men of the grand jury met on August 9, 1909, at nine o'clock and by two o'clock they had me charged with murder

The next day I was allowed to enter a plea. "Not guilty," I said to the judge.

Dad came to see me in jail as soon as he could get in from Thunder Hawk. He had hired some Aberdeen lawyers named Hazel and Huntington to defend me. Dad told the newspapers, "That boy is innocent of any crime. He was forced into shooting the other man by the necessity of defending himself, as both were intoxicated at the time and were not responsible for their actions. Those who were present at the shooting are confident that my son was not the aggressor and that his act could not be helped."

The newspapers went out of their way to note that Dad was a white man and that both Tom and I were "half-breed redskins." The *Aberdeen Daily News*, not being shy about its opinions, ran as a banner a headline "Redskin Charged with Killing Comrade," and offered two more subheads summing up its views, "Whiskey Cause of Killing," and added "Booze Cause of Killing" in case anybody missed the point the first time. They went on to say, "Booze is at the bottom of the killing, and it is possible that steps will be taken to prosecute the man who furnished the firewater to the breeds."

Later that same day the court got around to charging Ed Duncan with "introducing intoxicating liquors upon the Standing Rock Reservation." Some others were charged with that crime on different Sioux reservations. Next day all three cases was neatly disposed of. The *Aberdeen Daily News* specifically stated that the liquor introduced by Duncan was "that which made Gilland and Powers drunk and during which spree Gilland killed Powers." The newspapers had made up their minds, and they weren't too strong on either knowing all the facts or the idea of innocent until proven guilty if an Indian was involved.

I sat in that jail cell until the trial was finally held in November. Aberdeen was already crowded with people come in for the court session when Dad and Mother arrived. The railroads had been eagerly promoting South Dakota as the "coming" state for agriculture. Special trains from the east and south filled with land seekers had been coming into Aberdeen bringing people into the city for weeks. Extra coaches had been added and it was said that one hotel alone turned away a hundred people looking for a place to sleep. Families in search of a Dakota homestead were camped out in the Milwaukee Railroad depots. The railroads had land to sell cheap and the lottery drawings for reservation lands to be given away by Uncle Sam were just getting underway that year. Land that was settled and "improved" was soon worth a lot more to the railroads. Needless to say, the land seekers the railroad was trying to get to settle on Dakota land weren't ranchers and they sure weren't Lakota. And they weren't told that a quarter section of land wasn't anywhere near enough to support a family.

At the courthouse, there were some horse stealing cases and the three people were charged with selling liquor to Indians, but the central event was the "Gilland Murder Case." The town of Aberdeen had campaigned hard to get a November court session to be held there and they brought Judge Cartland up from Sioux Falls to preside.

The case of the *United States of America versus Robert Gilland* went to the jury at 5:30 in the evening on November 9, and three hours later, they found me guilty of willful murder. The twelve white men of the jury recommended a long prison term in the federal penitentiary rather than hanging. Two weeks later, Judge Cartland gave me life, eligible for parole in thirty years, and sent me to the federal prison in Leavenworth, Kansas, to serve out my sentence. On every one of the one thousand miles leading away from Thunder Hawk, I heard the train rails whispering to me. "You'll never see Lizzy again. You'll never see your family again."

After two days handcuffed to a train seat, I was checked into the federal penitentiary. It was the biggest building I had ever seen. Leavenworth's walls rose forty feet above the ground and were sunk forty feet below ground in case anybody thought of leaving before their time was up. The columned front of the prison was made of white stone pillars in a style I came to know was called "classical" like a Greek temple. It had only been open for a few years and inside the walls, there were still buildings being built. They made sure there was no shortage of hard work for prisoners to do.

Time moves in its own way when you have nothing but time. The first thing they did after they took me off the train in Kansas was to take my picture with my prison number on it. Everything that happened after that happened to that number, not a man named Red Eagle or one named Bob. About the only thing I was glad about was that I could read and write. That meant that I could hear from my family what was going on at home and I could read the papers and books about what was going on in the world. There was a big library and prisoners who followed all the rules, including no talking in chapel or in line going to dinner, got to read books and magazines from there. Leavenworth was a lot more comfortable than the county jail—it even had electric lights, flush toilets, and doctors to take care of people when they became sick.

I did make a few friends at Leavenworth, especially Big John. No one knew Big John's name, and if they spoke to him at all, it was "Big John." I had shared a cell with him and we got along great. He liked me and just acted like I was his little brother. The first night there at Leavenworth, I was put in a cell with Big John. Along about midnight (the inner cell doors were left open so we could all walk down the hall and use the one latrine on that cellblock), I was still wide awake. Big John had just went to the latrine, and three guys came a running in and one of them said, "Injun, we are all horny as hell and you is going to be our sweet ass tonight."

I said, "Not in your lifetime," and peeled out of bed and hit the one that had spoke, just as hard as I could and he went back hard and to the floor. The other two were grabbing at my arms, when Big John walked in. He grabbed a guy in each hand by the back of the neck and rammed them as hard as he could face-first into the cell bars, and without letting go, literally threw them down the hall. Then he reached down and picked up the one laying on the floor and smashed him into the cell bars too, and gave him a fling out in the hall.

Then he closed the cell door and turned and said, "I hate queers, and no one is going to cornhole anyone in my cell." Then he said, "We better get to bed pronto, before a guard comes a looking to see what the racket was about." I was in my bed and (at least pretending to be asleep) in less than two seconds. The next morning the guards came around and found those three horny dinks still a laying in the hall. Them guards sure started asking a lot of questions.

"I didn't hear or see anything. I was tired and I went right to sleep and never woke up until just now," I said. No one else talked either. Big John just gave them a mean glare, and the guards didn't even ask him a thing. They put me in solitary confinement for ten days trying to make me talk, but I figured, I'd rather eat bread and water for ten days than try to explain to Big John as to why I talked.

After ten days, the guards finally gave up on me talking and put me back in with Big John. He soon started talking to me and even told me his real name. I wouldn't even tell my own mother his real name because that is the way he wanted it. He told about working in a mine and being a lumberjack and working on the railroad for a while. He quit that job though. It seems one day the crew had to unload a load of eight-foot oak ties and carry them a ways down the track, and they had been just carrying one tie each. Then he said the foreman told them to double up on carrying those ties, so he carried two at a time for a while. Then that foreman said take five, so he carried five, but the second bunch of five, he just throwed down at the foreman's feet and quit. Said damned if he was going to carry that many. I wasn't sure if he was just kidding or if he really did carry that many ties, but I thought if anyone could carry five ties, it most likely would be Big John. He had said he had gotten life for killing a few skunks in a fight about ten years back, and I left it at that.

Dad wrote regularly at first. All my sisters and brothers and some others from back home kept on writing during those long years. There was never a letter from Lizzy, but I still kept writing to her for a while. I tried to write regular to everybody who wrote to me, but sometimes it was hard to know what to say. It helped my feelings when people wrote me that they knew I didn't kill Tom on purpose, but it didn't help my situation much.

Since I was sentenced to hard labor, that meant breaking up rocks in the "stone workshop." Some of the other boys in there told me they knew I didn't kill Tom. One said a friend of his had passed a word along to him through his sister, that when I got out I should go look up Arthur Vermillion and look him straight in the eye. "Don't say anything, just go look him in the eye when you get out." He didn't tell me the name of his sister's friend, but his description sure fit a certain Brave Bear I knew. At that time, I thought, well, that's fine but my chances of getting out of here while I could still walk anywhere were pretty slim.

Winter moved on and even in a Kansas prison spring comes. One day that first spring the warden called me in to say he got a letter from my mother asking if I was well or sick. I thought that was kind of funny since Mother couldn't write. The letter from "Mother" was written in my sister Bessie's hand. The next day the warden got a telegram from Dad saying,

> "Is Robert Gilland well or sick? Answer. Collect at once.
> Signed, Ben Gilland."

I guess the letter and telegram kind of lit a fire under the warden and he promptly sent a telegram back to Dad, saying "Robert Gilland is all right and working every day." He even wrote a letter to Mother that "your son works in the stone shop and is perfectly well. He has only been on sick call six times since he came here." It kind of helped that the warden knew I had a family that worried about me and wasn't a bad sort and he took an interest in my situation after that. I went up to his office again in July and asked him to send one of those photographs they took to Mother, and he did and sent her a nice letter with it.

Meanwhile, Dad with some help from Bessie, who was now studying at Carlyle College for Indians in Pennsylvania, started getting after the lawyers to get me a new trial. Those Aberdeen lawyers didn't do much for me at the trial but it seems that when they found out that I had some land of my own and how well they could get paid, they started acting more like lawyers.

Bessie helped find another law firm that even had offices in Texas who took my case. They brought it up through to the Supreme Court of the United States in Washington, DC. I guess Bessie had friends at that school from all over the country. Anyhow, I had to sell my land to pay them lawyers. All my money, my allotment payments, anything had to go through the Agency, and any letters regarding my money had to be handled by Warden McClaughry. Superintendent Belden of the Indian Agency keep pushing me to sell cheap, but the warden, he encouraged me to hold out for a fair price and wrote and told that cheapskate Belden so. Funny how people who are supposed to be on your side aren't and those who aren't turn out to be.

So after I'd been in Leavenworth for about a year, I sold my land for less than the $3,000 it was worth but I got enough to pay the Aberdeen lawyers, the Texas lawyers, and the application for a new trial. That spring the lawyers got a hearing set before the Supreme Court, which would consider my case in October.

I was waiting for October to come around, when I began to feel a little weak and started coughing a lot. I thought it was just the dust in the stone shop. Then I woke up during the night coughing and soaked through with sweat and cold all over at the same time.

"You best get to the doctor," said Big John when he couldn't sleep anymore because of my coughing. "It sounds like you got the TB." He started clanging on the cell bars until the guards came. They looked me over and agreed with Big John.

I was in the prison hospital for a couple of weeks and then in the TB Annex for a couple of months. In the TB Annex I slept in a big room with lots of beds like it was at Indian school. When I started getting better I got to do inside work for a while, and when I got stronger, they assigned me take care of the warden's horses. As the weather warmed, I worked in the cow barn and on building a new cell block building. That was sure a lot better than busting rocks.

While I was in the Annex recovering, the Supreme Court turned over the Circuit Court conviction and ordered a new trial. It seems that unlike a jury of white townsfolk in Aberdeen, the Supreme Court thought that Judge Cartland had played a little fast and loose with the facts about what had happened that night. If I was the one who killed Tom, I didn't mean to, and if I weren't the one, someone else needed to be facing the reach of the law. I always thought that nobody could had of "willfully, feloniously with malice aforethought commit the crime of murder" while drunk and sitting around with eight or ten other boys looking on.

The new lawyer, L. W. Crowfoot, even asked the warden for a health report, said he didn't want me waiting around in the Brown County jail until spring if I was still suffering from TB. The prison doctor wrote him saying that I had no signs or symptoms of TB and I'd returned to work. He even added that he thought being in prison had saved my life because I wouldn't have gotten good health care otherwise. That was taking a little too much credit, I thought, because if I hadn't been in prison, I probably wouldn't have gotten TB in the first place. In November, they took me back to Aberdeen, and I pled guilty to manslaughter and was sentenced to five years. I had to go back to Leavenworth, but I would be eligible for parole in July 1915.

Warden McClaughry made me a prison trusty in January, and that meant I didn't have to go back to busting rocks. After that, I worked in the barns mostly taking care of the prison's horses. That summer I signed some big checks to the lawyers and to Dad to pay the legal fees. During the next year, things were slow and quiet. Lawyer Crowfoot asked the doctors to give me a physical exam and they did and said I had no evidence of my "previous illness." Lawyer Crowfoot and the warden started the paperwork to get me paroled. About the only other thing that happened that year was I got a tooth filled, but they had to charge me a dollar for the filling and they even had to ask Belden for that buck! Then the warden had to write to that cheapskate again to get $50 so I could get some extra clothes for going home.

In July, I sent for some new clothes, the warden gave me a train ticket to Thunder Hawk, and I walked out a free man after six years and five months.

As they were taking me to the train station, the warden said one more thing, "A lot of young men are joining up to help fight the war in Europe. There's gonna be a draft for the army soon. This country won't be able to stay out of this war," he said.

"In that case, I'll just volunteer right now," I said. So I did, but they said they had to send me home and I would have to go from Thunder Hawk. I thought what a deal, well, let's head for that train station, then, I've had enough of Kansas!

I had plenty to think about on the train ride home. Mother had had Bessie write to me of the news at home while I was in

Leavenworth. Mother always signed her "X" on the letters. Lizzy had married a worthless character from over around Mobridge. Her dad liked Tom Powers and said his daughter wasn't going to get involved with a murderer. Lizzy never answered any of my letters either so I stopped writing them after a few years. I wondered if she had ever gotten them. Annie wrote and said that she heard that Lizzy had a little red-haired girl with slate-blue eyes. Now it was too late to matter anyway, but I wondered if she had gotten married in a certain pink dress.

When I got home, the Gilland land holdings were a lot smaller than they were when I went down to Leavenworth. Mother said now there were homesteaders on almost every quarter of land. Other things had changed a lot in those years too. People were getting gasoline-powered cars and trucks and tractors. More land was being plowed under every year for wheat and less was being used for cattle and horses. With the war in Europe, grain prices were high and a lot of horses were rounded up and shipped overseas.

Gilland family about 1915 on the porch of the homestead near Thunder Hawk built from the timbers hauled from Fort Yates. Left to right: Robert, Bessie, Elizabeth, and Benjamin.

The whole family was at the station in Thunder Hawk to meet me when I stepped from the train. When Mother threw her arms around me, I saw the long gray streaks in her tightly pulled-back bun. She was wearing high-heeled woman's shoes for the trip to town, but as soon as we got home, she would put on her moccasins as always. Dad's handlebar mustache and his hair were nearly all white, and he was wearing a bowler hat rather than the Stetson that had always been part of his looks to me. He chest was as barrel wide as ever, but his shoulders weren't soldier straight any more. Bessie had said in her last letter that he had been drinking quite a bit, and it showed in his face.

Abe had married Viola Kempton and was a father now, and had his wife and new baby girl there. Little Jimmie was most nigh six feet tall, and Bessie, well she was a full-grown woman now and a lot bigger than Mother. Jimmie said that Bessie's beau was one the white settlers, who'd moved down from Canada. Bessie had come back from Carlyle and would be teaching at the new grammar school. Not only was she a grown woman but a "modern" one. I'd seen a woman on the train with "bobbed hair," but I was surprised to see Bessie with her hair cut to just below her ears and wearing her skirt cut well above her ankles.

She laughed when she saw me gaping at her short hair and skirt, "Don't worry, Bob, I'm still wearing a skirt," and under her breath she whispered, "and a corset." In a louder voice she said, "All of us girls cut our hair after leaving Carlyle. It's so much more practical, and cooler too. Lots of farm and ranch girls prefer trousers now, though, I'm told," she teased. It would be a long time before I knew much about my sister's part in getting me back to Thunder Hawk.

Ben had been arrested for stealing horses and served a year in the county jail. Ben had wrote and said he got talked into going along with a certain half-breed friend of ours and the guy that had helped him trail horses home from Montana one time. I was certain who he meant. They went over east across the river and rounded up a bunch of horses and one white mule. Well, a lot of horses were chased across country and no one would have remembered, but everyone could remember seeing that white mule, and the law just tracked them horses right to his place. He got a year, mostly because he wouldn't tell who the other two were that had helped! Ed Duncan had got time too—two years—for giving us that whiskey. Charlie Gayton lost his sheriff job, and Annie had died at child birth with her sixth child.

Samie was there too. I shook his hand, and he said, "You come. I cook now, for whole family!" Samie was in cowboy boots and had on a Stetson and sure looked different than when I had first met him. He was head cook at the new Thunder Hawk café now. After a whale of a meal, at Samie's café, we all headed home and had a lot to talk about.

Dad said the reason I got a new trial had to do with Arthur going to the sheriff, saying his conscience started bothering him so he had to tell the truth. Dad said, "He told the sheriff that what the others had said about the fight was true and that Tom went for his gun first, and that I did warn him before I shot. He never said why he kept quiet so long."

Dad had spent a lot of his own money besides what I had on lawyers trying to get me out of Leavenworth. I sold my homestead and Dad sold his and a lot of the cattle herd to pay the lawyers. It seems that Bessie had learned some things about how to get along in the world while she was at Carlisle Indian College, and she had been writing letters and getting after the lawyers to work harder on my behalf. Bessie was determined to use the "advantages" she had to try to get me out. She always put Dad's name on the letters but she had picked up some back-east habits about how you get things done. And not giving up was one of them. She had Dad's stubbornness and no use at all for people with no gumption. When the new lawyers finally started doing their job, they started quizzing some of the boys who were there, and it seems that new evidence was turned up. Some pressure was likely added from somewhere else on the reservation too.

I'd been home a couple of days when I decided to ride out to Arthur's cabin down on the Cedar River. The back of a horse had never felt so good. His place was pretty shabby—all run down with broken-down corrals and junk laying around. Just like my Leavenworth friend-of-a-friend had said to, I knocked on the door. The door swung open, but I didn't go in. I just looked into that pair of hollow eyes and got back on my horse without saying a thing.

Arthur was found hanging in his shack a few days later with a note he wrote saying he just couldn't live with what he had done.

I couldn't help but wonder why, after so many years, all of a sudden did a person's conscience start bothering him. I would lay odds that Brave Bear might have helped him find his memory of that August night on the trail. They might of had a heart-to-heart talk, and Arthur had a choice, either tell the truth or face Brave Bear. And the hanging, that would be Brave Bear's way. I could never tell anyone what I thought was true, but I sure will try to make it up to him somehow when I get a chance!

No one at home had said much about Brave Bear so I had thought he was probably laying low somewhere. He wasn't much for writing but he would have known I was coming home. Ben had been at Fort Yates getting a wagonload of supplies, when he pulled up to the homeplace going a lot faster than was good for a wagon loaded with groceries.

He climbed down quickly, but there was a long silence before he spoke. Then Ben said, "Bob, your friend Brave Bear won't be coming to see you. He was heading toward Thunder Hawk and the law found out his whereabouts and set a trap at a bend of the Cedar River about fifteen miles northeast of town. He rode right down into the trees to ford the river and they had a posse of fifty or so men waiting up on the other side. Some said he tried to surrender but they just kept pumping lead into him anyway."

He stood silent for a few more minutes. "When I heard in town what had happened, some of us told the sheriff that we would take care of burying him. So we took his body up on a bluff overlooking the Missouri a little ways to the south. But instead of digging a grave, we built a scaffold and laid his body out in some cottonwood trees and so his spirit could find *mahpiya* (heaven). He would not have wanted a grave in the ground that could be found."

"Damned," I said without hesitation. "He didn't deserve to die that way." I suppose though that would have been the way he would have wanted to go, or feared of going. He had good reason to never trust the law. He was one of the most honest and loyal friends I'll ever have, and in my mind he is the reason I'm free today. I could not say it aloud, but I knew he was probably heading back from Vermillion's place when they caught him out in the open.

Ake wancinyankin ktelo, takola (good-bye, my best friend), Brave Bear.

EPILOG

On the Train to Fort Sam Houston

All the family were at the Thunder Hawk station with me again while we waited for the early morning train that would take me south to Texas. This time we were there to say good-bye not hello. But nobody said much, as we hovered against the chill around the station's potbellied stove. Dad knew the life of a soldier and although he would rather have me at home, he thought it might be for the best. Besides, lots of other boys from around the area were joining up too. The newspapers said it would be a short war once America joined in, and I kinda liked the idea of going someplace I'd never been.

"I know you will be a *akicita ohitika* (brave soldier)," Mother said. "Write to your father as often as you can."

I promised that I would and that I'd be back when this war in Europe was over. I would sure miss everyone at home, but with my land and cattle sold, Lizzy lost to me, and Brave Bear dead, I was glad to be heading out of Thunder Hawk for a new but unknown life in the army.

After I'd settled into my seat for the trip south, I thought the train must be doing most nigh thirty miles an hour, but we had to stop at every town for wood and water. It couldn't go fast enough for me getting out of Kansas City. I'd had too much of Kansas and I was anxious to get on to Fort Sam Houston and army training. We were rolling along just outside of Kansas City, when this tall drink of water, stands up and bellers, "Back where I come from, you let ladies have your seat when there aren't any others available!" I'd been dozing off and hadn't been paying much attention, but there were two ladies standing in the aisle and all the seats were already taken.

The tall fellow—seems his name was "Slim"—was only a few seats ahead of where I was sitting, and I could see that he was looking at the passenger sitting next to where he'd been a sitting. That hombre sitting down smirked out, "I ain't about to let some black wench have my seat!"

I hadn't even noticed, but now that he mentioned it, the gals standing there were maybe breed blacks, but they sure weren't dark like the blacks back at prison. A few blacks who'd run away from slavery and had made as far north as Indian territory in the early days were just accepted by different tribes for who they were. Later, after the Civil War, some went west and just settled in with the Indians, and well eventually, just like some Indians were lighter, some were darker. Anyway, they were well dressed and pretty gals. I couldn't see any need to be rude to them.

This Slim had a really long reach, and he just reached over and grabbed that fellow right by the top of the head and raised him out of his seat in less than a split second. The gals looked kind of scared and one of them spoke in almost a whisper, "We don't want any trouble, we'll just stand!" Slim acted like he didn't even hear the gal, he just pulled the fellow right out in the aisle by his hair and they headed for the door at the opposite end of this passenger car. They went by me at a fast pace, and two other fellows came a scampering along behind them that I figured were friends of the first gent.

Well, Mother raised her sons to always respect women and Dad raised us to try to keep a fight fair, so I came up kinda fast and moved right along too. About the time they were catching up to Slim, I tapped one of them lads on his shoulder and he turned around quick and looked a little surprised. I didn't say anything, just gave him a very hard left jab and he sat down right behind Slim and the other fellow, who had grabbed Slim by his free arm, but Slim just shook him loose and had him by the hair too. Out on the platform the three went, and Slim gave the first a boot in the rear end as he went sailing off the train and the other one went the same way but off the opposite side of the platform. Then Slim came back through the door as the one sitting there was just getting his bearings back and helped him to his feet by grabbing the back of his collar, and he too was soon making a quick exit from the train.

I headed back to my seat but before I got there a big hand was on my shoulder and as I turned around, a voice said softly, "Thanks, friend! I'm John Summers, but most call me Slim." We shook hands and that was the beginning of a long friendship.

Everybody else on the train was trying to act nonchalant, some even pretended to be sleeping. The girls had already taken two of the vacant seats, so Slim and I took the other two and I was soon learning some about John Summers. As it happened, his brother, Jessie who had come into the Dakotas with the latest bunch of homesteaders, had a homestead four miles east of Thunder Hawk, and Slim was helping him out when he decided to volunteer for the army. He'd been a mule skinner in Missouri, but he liked it out west and figured one day would make his home there, after he got back from the army. The war in Europe was heating up and lots of boys from all over were joining up, including some of the boys I'd known since Indian school, like Felix Fly and Harry Fast Horse. The newspapers said the United States would soon be in the fight. Slim had gone back to Missouri to visit his folks, mostly to tell them about a gal he had met over south of Thunder Hawk, Alma Pearson, before heading for army training in Texas. I had a feeling just by the way he said her name that I very probably would be a hearing a lot more about Alma before we got home. I told him that we'd probably end up in the same army outfit, as that's where I was headed too.

"I beg your pardon," the gal sitting across from us spoke, and was looking mostly at me so I figured she was wanting to talk. Then she asked if they could treat us to a lunch or a drink. "There's a café car next car up front and we would like to thank you gents for being so nice to us."

"Sure," I answered back, but you don't owe us anything." The girls got up and headed for the café car, and I got up too and followed along. I wasn't so sure about Slim but we were soon all four sitting at a dining table and looking at a menu.

The gal sitting to my right, spoke up first with, "Before we order, I think we should all introduce ourselves. I'm Mariah McKulah," and she offered her hand.

"I'm Robert Gilland, most call me Bob, but some call me Red Eagle," I said as I shook her hand.

Then Slim had his turn at hand shaking, and the other gal interrupted with, "And I'm Rosie Smith. We've been visiting our families in Kansas City, but we're going back to Tulsa, Oklahoma. We both got jobs in a factory there." The waiter came around about then and we all ordered a meal. I thought, no way am I going to let these pretty little gals pay for my meal! The train was really a rolling along now, and we should be up to Tulsa by late this evening. But we'd have to switch trains there and catch the one heading south to Texas. We all went back to our seats and they were still vacant; we must have been talking for the last six hours to Mariah and Rosie.

When we pulled into Tulsa, it was late at night but time sure goes fast when you get caught up in conversation. The depot agent said, "Boys, your train west won't be leaving here until ten tomorrow morning, so you just as well head on over to a hotel for the night, get a good night's rest, and be back before ten tomorrow."

I looked at Slim, and he suggested we do as the agent had said, or else we would be trying to sleep in the depot on hard benches. We had bid the gals good-bye when we went into the depot, but they were still standing outside when we came out of the depot. Mariah spoke first (she seemed to always speak first), "Why don't you help us carry our bags home—we have an extra bed and a cot. You all can just as well stay at our place, we only live six blocks away, and we'll make sure you are up in plenty of time to catch the train in the morning." I didn't have to ask Slim what he wanted to do, he already had a bag in one hand and Rosie on the other arm. I just followed suit, and Mariah took my arm and we were off.

We were soon at their rooming house, which was up some stairs, off a quiet street. Mariah, almost in a whisper, said, "You must be tired too, let's just head for bed," and she led me to a bedroom and closed the door and started to shed her clothes, so I just did too. It had been a long dry spell for me and Mariah sure broke the drought. Well, we made it back to the train on a run, all the while I'm a thinking that Mariah had kisses sweeter than wine.

Soon I'll be off to fight a real war. My pay started when I passed the physical so I'm in the army now and in the money too, almost sixty cents a day. I'm thinking, a new chapter in my life is about to begin, and I really hope it turns out better than the last one.

About the Authors

George Gilland, a member of the Standing Rock Sioux Tribe, is a direct descendant of Robert Gilland. He has raised prize-winning cattle on the Standing Rock Sioux Reservation for more than thirty years and has won several grand championship trophies for breeding Red Galloways and Blonde d'Aquitaines, and for hard riding in Team Penning contests. He has served as President of the Lakota Ranchers Association and Treasurer of the American Indian Livestock Association.

Sharon Rasmussen's ancestors and family lived on the Standing Rock Sioux Reservation through much of her childhood. She is the granddaughter of Elizabeth Gilland Fero. She has been a technical writer, feature writer, and editor for more than thirty years and is President of Polestar Consulting, LLC, providing editorial services to organizations in Washington, D.C. Ms. Rasmussen holds a B.A. cum laude from Wesleyan University and an M.Ed. from George Mason University. Mr. Gilland and Ms. Rasmussen are cousins as well as co-authors.